THE VALLEY OF AMERICAN SHADOW

Gregg Voss

ISBN: 978-0-578-52969-1

Library of Congress Control Number: 2019908699

For Dorothy and Emmie

"Everything can be explained, but not everything can be understood."

—Rabbi Menachem Eisenstein

PATIENCE

Edmund, Kansas

There was no air conditioning in the Edmund School office. That was a luxury other districts could afford, like the one in Lawrence where Molly Driscoll had completed her student teaching the prior spring. *No,* she thought, *I'm in rural Kansas, farm country, amber waves of grain, and all that. Grassroots America.* Molly pondered this while using her front teeth to massage a canker sore on the tip of her tongue. The sultry early September summer air from the school office's only open window seemingly hung over her head like a coming storm.

Molly was sitting on a hardwood chair outside Principal Mamie Kroupa's office because of Patrick. He was the wild one, if any of the students at Edmund School could be considered wild. It was remarkable—for seventh graders, no less—that they sat attentively in her English and social studies classes with hands folded, the girls in their plaid uniform skirts and the boys in white polos. They grinned as if they knew something she didn't, but gave her nary a problem. The kids turned in their assignments on time, and their test and quiz scores were, so far anyway, more than acceptable. In other words, a first-year teacher's dream, which contrasted with the missives of her KU professors about the imperative of establishing disciplinary procedure on day one, and then following through as necessary.

"Expect to follow through," they'd said. "A lot."

Control. That's what classroom management was all about she was told: maintaining control. But Molly sometimes wondered who was really in control of her classroom.

Patrick maybe was the only exception. Just maybe. True, he did drop a pseudo-smart ass comment during fifth period yesterday, but it had actually made Molly smile inwardly. In truth, it was sort of refreshing to have a middle schooler act like a middle schooler, rather than managing a group of kids who looked like they were attending a sales seminar. She'd shrugged off Patrick's comment, which had sounded like a thinly veiled attempt to challenge another teacher's intelligence. To Molly, it didn't warrant follow-through; she hadn't even given it a second thought. Sometimes discretion really is the better part of valor.

Patrick arrived in homeroom the next morning with a cast on his right hand and a black eye. And was that a limp Molly noticed? She asked the handsome boy with the brown, wavy hair and long fingers, like a pianist's, to stay after class for a few minutes. But he had been reticent, mumbling something about not wanting to be late to first-period math. But Molly picked and pried a little, wheedling him with a compliment about his 100% score on the American government quiz. But then again, all of her students got 100. *Uncanny*. Maybe she wasn't making her measurements tough enough.

"What happened to you, Patrick?" Molly finally asked, motioning toward his hand.

His pause was deafening, and the response was weak willed, beaten. "It happened on the farm," he said, eyes drooping toward the textbooks in his left hand.

"Really?" Molly replied. "Because I think it was something else, and I want to help you. This looks pretty serious, and if another student hurt you, we need to take care of that. I'm going to talk to Miss Kroupa about this, and maybe…"

"No. No!" Patrick fairly wailed at the prospect. "You can't. Please don't talk to Miss Kroupa." Then a half shrug as if to say, *You'll make it worse.*

After another pause, he held up his casted right hand and said, "This will heal, and everything will be fine. I'll do better. You'll see." An unconvincing, dubious smile and he left. Molly's classroom was silent.

I'll do better.

Molly rolled that phrase around in her mind as she concentrated for a moment on her canker sore and looked down at her sensible black flats. If Patrick had been beaten up—but for what? certainly not what he'd said in class, that didn't seem plausible—then it needed to be handled, and that might get messy, especially if a parent had been involved. Especially a parent out here.

On one of her in-service days, she walked into school humming a Jay-Z tune, and a group of parents were clucking outside the main office. As she walked by, they stopped and stared at her and picked up their conversation in hushed tones as she ambled down the hall, still watching warily.

Miss Mamie Kroupa's office door opened. "Miss Driscoll, I understand you need to speak to me?" she said. "Please, come in."

The chilled air from Miss Kroupa's window air conditioner socked Molly in the face as she walked in and found another hardwood seat in front of an elegant oak desk, stained chocolate brown. Molly had admired it ever since she interviewed for her current position in July, and Miss Kroupa apparently noticed.

"This was Daddy's," she said, as she rolled her finger along the desk, referring to her father, Edmund Kroupa, the school's namesake. "He was the principal here for nearly forty years, bless his soul. He made this school, and this town, what it is today. She proudly gestured to a sepia photo on the wall of a dour man in a suit. It was next to a carved wooden plaque with a single word: *Patience*.

Miss Kroupa was both dowdy and corpulent, and the springs of her leather chair whined as she eased her girth into it. She was dressed in a long flowery dress, vaguely Amish, and her ashen curls looked a little like a bird's nest—or maybe even a wig. No wedding ring or anything else, like a necklace or a bracelet, that suggested femininity. Molly secretly suspected Miss Kroupa was a lesbian, which was exacerbated by the fact that she seemed to be staring at Molly's slightly erect nipples due to the coolness of the room.

"What can I do for you, Miss Driscoll?" Miss Kroupa finally said, making a show of sitting up in her chair.

"Well," Molly started, with a conviction that sounded naïve as that first word crossed her lips, "I'm concerned about one of my students, Patrick Powers, who came to school today with a black eye and a cast on his hand. He said it had happened on his family's farm, but I don't know if that's true. It might have been an after-school fight, but based on the behavior I've seen from my students so far, I doubt it. Which leaves a few possibilities, but one in particular troubles me."

The implication hung in the air, and Miss Kroupa leaned back in her chair to consider it for a long while. "What would you have me do, Miss Driscoll?" she finally said.

"Well if a parent were involved, doesn't that warrant an investigation?" Molly countered. "I mean, he's pretty beaten up. A black eye is one thing. But a broken hand, it looks like, is something else."

"Yes, I saw him in the hallway earlier," Miss Kroupa's voice trailed, turning her attention to the plaque. "Pity. But I'm not sure there is much we, as a school, can do."

Molly had a student back in Lawrence, another seventh-grade boy she suspected was being abused by his father, and after a long talk, her supervising teacher got the school social worker involved. One-two-three and Daddy-o was arrested by the Lawrence PD and charged with battery, among other things. So she knew protocol.

"We don't have a social worker in this county," Miss Kroupa said, folding her hands on the desk as if to emphasize the point. "As you've probably already surmised, this isn't a wealthy area like Topeka or Wichita or even Lawrence. For wont of a better phrase, we may as well be on an island. We tend to take care of our problems ourselves."   Then she gestured at the plaque and said, "We use patience. Daddy believed in patience, and it has served us well for decades."

Molly shifted in her seat, the wood smooth and warming under her plaid skirt. It took a few seconds for the thoughts in her mind to coalesce into a cohesive response, but it did command Miss Kroupa's attention. She took a breath and forged onward. "With respect, Miss Kroupa, being patient may not be an appropriate response or in the best interest of the boy," Molly said. "What if Patrick goes home tonight and gets hurt again or worse? Wouldn't we—this school and its staff, including you and me—be liable if we suspected something was wrong and didn't report it?"

"Report to whom, exactly?" Miss Kroupa said, then made a grand effort to stand, pushing her chair away so that it banged against the credenza behind her. "The police and the town fathers endorse patience and know it's this school's virtue."

She noticed Molly's blank stare, hobbled over to the desk's corner, and leaned against it. Molly could smell Miss Breck hairspray, which immediately took her back years ago to the bathroom in her grandmother's house in Kansas City. She brushed that thought away, as if the mingling of the two was somehow sour.

"You're thinking of patience as a noun, my dear," Miss Kroupa went on, placing fat fingers with stubby, unpainted nails on Molly's knee. "*Here,* patience is a verb." Another blank stare. Miss Kroupa went on, treading without apparent empathy. "You may not realize it quite yet, but you've been given a wonderful gift by joining the staff at this school: a job for the rest of your career and a salary commensurate with performance—provided you embrace patience."

Molly hadn't planned to spend any more time at Edmund School than was absolutely necessary. She only wanted to pay her dues and then move on to a more palatable job situation back home in Kansas City or Lawrence. Job availability was scarce without the requisite experience, and naturally, you can't gain experience without a job beyond student teaching. She felt confident she would be able to make that move after a year or two. But layoffs were a constant concern, especially in the urban and suburban districts. In fact, after fifteen years, her supervising teacher had gotten the axe at the conclusion of the school year.

"Find a spot where you can grow," were his parting words after Molly had cleaned out her desk. "Find a spot, and maybe not even in Kansas, where you can practice your craft and make a difference without worrying about budget cuts all the time. You owe that to yourself and the kids."

With that advice top of mind, Molly had accepted the position at Edmund School. Country bumpkins might not be so focused on bean counting, she surmised, and plus, she didn't have to stay long term. Just long enough.

Now things were changing. Guaranteed career employment?

"You are a very talented, very bright teacher," Miss Kroupa went on. "I saw that in your résumé, your letters of recommendation, and your interviews this summer. Frankly, you are the kind of teacher Daddy used to hire because those teachers never let him down. They prepared our children for the eventuality of being contributing citizens to this county."

Which was funny to Molly because in a casual conversation with her homeroom students on the first day of school, now two weeks ago, about their career goals, the invariable answer was: "Work on the farm." Not that farming wasn't a noble profession, mind you, it's just that their apparent intellectual capabilities and collective demeanor suggested that they were capable of more. Perhaps a lot more, like even positions of leadership at the highest levels of public- or private-sector entities.

Kind of seemed like kids who could change the world someday. If they wanted to.

Check that. If they were allowed to.

"Your opportunity stands before you," Miss Kroupa said. "A long, happy career of fostering the educational path of some of the brightest children in this state, while being able to pursue your own ends without concern for losing your source of income."

Molly flashed to the KU School of Education graduation party that spring outside of Pearson Hall complete with streamers, gifts, well wishes and free-flowing booze. She gazed once again at the smiling faces so full of promise, and was forced to admit Miss Kroupa might be right. How many of her fellow graduates were working as baristas or bartenders or anything other than the educators they were trained to be? And for the ones who did make it into the workforce, how many would soon become acquainted with the pink slip, as her own father used to say?

Miss Kroupa lifted her girth from the corner of the desk, which made a creaking noise much like a sigh of relief. She took two steps to her left and positioned herself next to the carved wooden plaque that read Patience.

"This word," she said with a vigorous shake of her head, "this word is what Daddy relied on to maintain order in this school, especially when that vile rock and roll made its ugly appearance in the 1950s and when our students tried to rebel against authority a decade later. Through it all, even the advent of the Internet and its myriad temptations, patience has been our guiding principle. And as I said, here in this place, it is a verb, not a noun."

Miss Kroupa met Molly's eyes with her own, and they bored into her with electric arc-like precision.

"Are you willing to learn about patience?" Miss Kroupa asked. "Are you willing to learn and understand and join us in creating something wonderful here at Edmund School, the perfect educational environment?" Another pause. "If your answer is yes, then please follow me."

Molly turned her head and didn't move. Miss Kroupa seemed to glide behind her, and she placed her pudgy palms on Molly's shoulders and whispered in her ear: "Come along, Molly. You know in your heart this is the only way."

Molly's upper body tensed. She pulled forward and wrenched her body away from the hands that she realized were warm and possibly even perspiring.   "Miss Kroupa, this is *not* appropriate, and…" Molly began before Miss Kroupa dismissed her with a wave that signified a great big pshaw, to use a term from Edmund Kroupa's era.

"An effective educational environment requires order from the top on down, from myself and the board of education to the lowliest student in your classroom, like young Mr. Powers," she said, her tone now hard-nosed with resolve and fervency. "Think of this school as a complex ecosystem that is always a hair's breadth away from collapse if steps aren't taken to ensure order on a daily basis. Can we at least establish that?"

Molly found it hard to argue that point. She had been told as much in her KU educational theory classes, which is where she learned about classroom management and following through as required.

Miss Kroupa continued, "Daddy believed there was only one way to maintain that perfect state of order and that's patience. Order requires—I daresay demands—patience, and it's what you must learn to become a respected faculty member here. The parents of these children, all of whom make up our board of education and this town's civil servants, are depending on you to do just that." She thrust her sausage-like forefinger into Molly's left shoulder, which made Molly wince a little.

"You keep talking about patience, that it's a verb, not a noun," Molly said. "But what does that mean?"

"A fair question," Miss Kroupa said. "I'd rather show you than tell you. If you really want to take that step into a larger world, a veritable educational utopia, please follow me."

Miss Kroupa opened her office door and waddled past her secretary, Miss Marsh, who didn't even look up from what she was doing.

"Patience is really about the future," she said as Molly fell in step next to her, the two striding down the main hallway toward the rear of the school and the verdant acreage beyond. "This town, this county can't afford mass exodus of its population, or it will die. Our best and brightest must remain, and in some cases, like that of Mr. Powers, they must be compelled."

Molly could see the black-robed figures through the windows of the back door, their hands clutching what looked like rubber truncheons.

She pushed open the left door with a metallic thud, and under a blazing Indian summer sun stood a terrified fifth-grade girl she only knew as Kayla. The blonde in knee socks and a plaid skirt was being held by two robed, masked figures, one of whom Molly believed was the kindergarten teacher Mrs. Tatum, because of the long, red nails that emerged through bell-bottom sleeves. Ten other teachers, presumably, also masked and robed, formed two lines.

"Mr. Powers thought he'd like to leave this county and attend Kansas State to become a musician," Miss Kroupa said. "Patience made him see otherwise. As for Miss Kayla here, she had harbored notions of becoming a doctor, but the economic downturn of the last decade did considerable harm to the prospects of her father's farm. Patience is the only thing that will ensure she stays and fulfills her duty to her family."

Miss Kroupa held up her forefinger and whipped it from left to right. The robed figures holding Kayla forced her between the two lines and then pushed her forward. She began to run and cowered as the blows rained down. She finally curled up on the ground as each robed figure made a strike with their baton. The young girl's blonde hair was suddenly streaked pink and then red due to a cut on her forehead.

Kayla lay motionless on the shaggy grass, and Molly could vaguely hear whimpering and indistinguishable blather. It had all happened so quickly that she was stunned.

Molly turned to Miss Kroupa, who was staring proudly at the spectacle. Before she could move, the two robed figures who had been restraining Kayla now huskily grabbed each of Molly's arms. Apparently her colleagues. "Patience is our virtue, Miss Driscoll," Miss Kroupa said. "If you are to become one of us, you must learn it, embrace it, and realize it ensures our survival…and yours."

Molly noticed her canker sore had started to bleed, and with an iron taste in her mouth, the robed figures dragged her toward the two lines that had reformed.

PAYDIRT

Sanpoil, Washington

Coach Randy Mace was a wild-eyed preacher, a sidelines evangelist who exhorted his tiny congregation of eleven, including me, with a puffed chest and colorful language.

"You see that scoreboard?" he shrieked, bouncing his headset into the snowy grass and pointing toward the north end of the field, his finger quivering. It was getting dark, and the pale-yellow numbers were more pronounced in the dusky late afternoon. "You see it?"

Sure, I saw it. Everyone did: Visitors 10. Home 7.

Fourth down. Ten yards to go. Ball on our own thirty-seven-yard line.

Most troubling, if you're into football: 0:04 remaining.

"I'm not going out this way *again!*" coach said, placing undue emphasis on that last word, pronouncing it something like "uhhh-gain." It was hard to blame him; Forreston had knocked his teams out of the Class 1A state playoffs five times in his twenty-one years as Sanpoil High's head coach.

But this time was different. This time, a trip to state hung in the balance.

What am I doing here? I mean, I'm just rank freshman Riley Rathman, and I don't even like football much. I'm more for theater, drama, even choir. "Fairy stuff," my dad says. I don't hate football, mind you, but when you're 6-foot-1, 182 pounds, can run like a deer, and your dad was the school's big star back in the day, you play football. Period.

"We're going to win this on Colton's arm," Coach Mace went on, shifting his finger from the scoreboard to his only son, the star quarterback, and the closest thing in my life to a supervillain. "All we need is to get into field goal range. You can do this. You *hafta* do this!"

I had my doubts. I shifted my eyes to Colton, who like most of his senior teammates saw freshman as nothing but tackling dummies and targets for pranks and insults. It had been that way since the first practice back in August. A deluge of condescension and nasty comments. I took it; like I said, I'm just a rank freshman.

Colton had gotten up slowly after the last play and didn't seem to be all there, like he was dizzy or something. His head was down as he came off the field, and when he lifted it up toward the graying sky, he was wincing. Our trainer, Lizzie, started toward him but was waved off by Coach, as if he didn't want to contemplate the fact that his season could end without his son on the field.

"C'mon, Colt, snap out of it," he said, grabbing him by the shoulder pad and shaking him. Which didn't help whatever was up with Colton's head, probably a concussion.

He gritted his teeth through the double bars of his facemask. But he couldn't let his dad down. Not now. Not ever.

Just like me.

"We're going to 'Go Flash,' and get this one into OT," Coach said with adamant resolve, referring to a long sideline pass to another senior, receiver Jeff Farina, who wasn't as big a bastard as Colton, but in the same area code. With any luck—a lot of it, actually—he'd catch it and dart out of bounds. Farina's brother, Nate, was our kicker and was pretty solid from about thirty yards out. Thus, we had to get to about Forreston's twenty with a chance to tie.

Anything less and this one would go down as perhaps the biggest disappointment in Sanpoil's football history. And Coach would grouse about it all winter and spring, probably sending out emails with the subject line: "Do you want a repeat of the state semis? Better start lifting!" He'd take it out on Colton, who was a surefire collegiate Division III talent and was being eyed up by Wisconsin-Whitewater, among other power schools. But his dad wanted him to get that scholarship to a Division I school, maybe Washington State or Oregon State. A win here and a solid performance at the state finals, and that was guaranteed. According to Coach, of course, and my dad.

I'll admit that I had no business being on the field at that moment, and frankly, I didn't want to be. But our starting running back, senior Dylan Morgan, broke his leg in the first half on a jet sweep right in front of our sideline. Our other two backs, the Schneider twins, both stood 5-foot-8 and maybe 135 pounds, so they weren't an option when it came to blocking.

So that left me, a freshman fourth stringer. I had the girth, if not the strength. I was a drone, a hole filler, the only option.

"Hey freshman," Coach bellowed. "You have one job to do. *One!* Take out any linebacker crossing the line of scrimmage. All you have to do is protect Colton. Give him a chance to throw the ball. Think you can do that?"

I was listening, but in the north end zone, under the scoreboard and apparently on the edge of the field, there was something. Someone. There, under the scoreboard, maybe even in the far edge of the end zone.

"Hey!" Coach's voice cut through the late-afternoon gloom. "Are you listening, freshy? Are you focused? This is for everything… Dammit, how do I get stuck with these knuckleheads?"

I quietly apologized, but I don't think he heard me because he was already in his son's facemask. "Under no circumstances is the freshman to get the ball. If you get flushed, run for it and get out of bounds with time on the clock. If freshy gets the ball, this one's over. You read me? I'd rather have you take the sack than lose because a freshman ended up with the ball." He threw a nasty look in my direction.

A whistle and we trotted back onto the field. Out of the corner of my eye I saw the figure again. It was a woman with a long, flowing dress; a blue apron; puffy sleeves; and a beehive hairstyle.

She was beckoning me toward her as if to confide in me.

I lined up in the I-formation behind Colton and his line, made up of guys who've played together since the lower grades. I had no real affinity for them, though I could appreciate the fact that they were facing almost certain elimination. I had three years yet, if I chose to keep playing. There was my dad and his desire to live vicariously through his son.

My hands were on my bent knees, and I could barely see over the line, but the odd woman was still there, a sort of light-green aura enveloping her body. But then opposing linebacker #54, the brutal corn-fed lug who'd broke Dylan's leg, shifted position and blocked her from view.

"Red…ninety-eight! Red…ninety-eight!" Colton called.

"Come," came a quiet voice somewhere in front of me, over the din of near-men ready for combat.

"Set…"

Again the voice with urgency this time. *"Come."*

"Go!"

I was half a step slow, still basically standing still when Colton faked the handoff. I immediately looked for #54, and there he was, coming up through our line with a full head of steam. I winced and lowered my center of gravity, hoping to hit him low.

But at the last second, the hole was filled by a big blob with a dark jersey—one of ours. And here's where I went wrong. Or was it right? I don't know. I just reacted.

I cut to outside to the left instead of looking for someone else to block.

Colton was getting flushed from the pocket. I learned later that Farina was in double coverage, and no other options available, so he went to his safety valve.

Me.

"Aaaaugghhh!" came an anguished cry from the sideline. Coach Mace.

Let me be clear, I didn't *want* the ball. Ever. But it was a perfect throw. Floated right into my numbers. I caught it, juggled it for the briefest of moments, and then turned up the field.

"Come." There she was, sliding into my field of vision, but this time her hands over her head like Notre Dame's "Touchdown Jesus."

She became my beacon, my singular focal point as I headed up the field, dashing past a diving #54, who recovered from his block nicely.

"Oh, no! No! Anybody but him!" Coach Mace screamed.

Suddenly, the entire world was chasing me. I darted toward the Forreston sideline and could see the shadows of dark lines forming on the face of its head coach as I sailed by. He knew something I didn't, something behind me. Turns out, when my dad and I watched the replay of the game later, there had been a breakdown in the defensive backfield. Guys were chasing me, but when they got within a yard or two, they inexplicably fell.

"Come."

I glanced from her to the clock, which now read 0:00. *Now or never.* And then a new signal: footsteps came up fast on my right side, a hand on my shoulder, and a hard yank of my jersey made me spin around. I lost sight of her and nearly stepped out of bounds.

It was #54, and for a split second I marveled at his speed. I was regaining my footing—my dark jerseys too far away to help—when he lunged at me. But he bounced off of me; I can't say it any other way. He just hit the grass with a thud and rolled behind me. I didn't even feel anything, just a light touch that felt like a push.

The last twenty yards were a blur, but I homed in on her once again. This time, she was holding both of her hands out as if she was going to grab mine and welcome me, like a mother might greet a child who had come home after a long journey. When I crossed the end zone, I didn't jump up or bounce around like you see the NFL or college players on TV. No, I just sank into the grass, next to her, and closed my eyes, overcome with emotion.

When I opened them, she was gone.

We went to state and won a close one: 17-13 over Colville. Colton was the MVP and ended up getting a "preferred walk on" offer from the University of Washington. Not a scholarship, but he could work toward it. Coach Mace was named Coach of the Year by the Associated Press and other prestigious state media. All the talk was about the father-and-son duo who had overcome years of heartbreak to win it all. It made for a good story. Which was fine with me.

That big play in the semis was the last down of football I played. I didn't go out my sophomore year, deciding to try out for the school play, *Oklahoma!,* instead. I was happy to win the lead role of Curly McLain. "Pansy," my father said with a wink, but I wondered how much he was joking, since I'd crushed his football dream.

In preparing for my role, I learned that Sanpoil High had put on *Oklahoma!* several times before, the first time in 1963. I dug up the 1963 yearbook in the school library and thumbed through it, finally settling on the two-page spread that showed a gaggle of photos of that year's production.

And there she was. On page 47, lowermost photo on the right side of the page, barely visible. It was Laurey, the female lead *and* the woman I saw on the football field that day.

In 1963 Laurey Williams had been played by someone named Linda Mace, a senior who was a member of the Glee Club, choir, and the National Honor Society.

Linda. Coach Mace's older sister. Colton's aunt.

Linda had died in a car crash the following fall as a freshman on her way to a University of Washington football game.

TRENDING

Carson, California, a Los Angeles suburb

Two years ago

The boy had a pencil. A *pencil*. He gripped the weathered blue stub with his thumb and forefinger, his body heat warming the wood and the graphite within, the indentation of the manufacturer's name long worn off. There wasn't much of a tip, and the eraser was a nub, but still, it was a writing utensil.

It was like finding gold. A just reward for an hour's worth of covertly mining the garbage heap on the edge of town, all while avoiding patrolling occupiers, both real and holographic. It was becoming harder to tell the difference, but regardless, a chance meeting in that position would have resulted in a trip downstate to the reeducation camp near Escondido.

A pen would have been better, of course, but those had been outlawed when martial law was declared in greater Los Angeles by the occupiers, what, five years ago, now? During the Great Confiscation—when everyone was required to give up their computers, phones, and every other electronic communication device—all the paper, pens, and pencils had also been taken. In the wake of that, some had written notes in blood on ripped clothing as a less-than-casual response, usually communiqués to family members elsewhere in the city, but when they were eventually caught, they were sent downstate.

And nobody came back from the reeducation camps.

"What?" his mother thundered as he hunkered at the kitchen table after she carefully closed the curtains over the sink to avoid indiscreet eyes. "Where did you get that?"

It made no sense to palm the pencil or try to conceal it. Somehow mothers have always known the goings on within the four walls of their homes since time eternal, even if illicit activities were just beyond their sight. This was no different and, of course, he had promised her he wouldn't bring home anything to write with, but what have kids always done? Rebel.

His mom had been a striking woman before the occupation, blonde hair fashionably trimmed to her shoulders, manicured nails, pumps, and a confident gait. There was still a hint of those days in her trussed hair, but it was graying to match her current pallor. A lime-green housecoat masked the weight she had gained from the occupiers' grain-heavy diet, lack of exercise thanks to curfew (she had been an early morning or evening runner), and, of course, the death of her husband at the hands of the occupiers after they had first arrived. Just for being a community college professor.

She tried to grab the pencil from the boy's hand, but he moved at the last minute and held it in the air as if it were a bauble or, perhaps, a talisman. Something immensely valuable, which it was. To him anyway. Gold. To her, it was something darker, dangerous. A shadow in the mist.

She sat down. They stared at each other for a long moment, and she measured her words. "You know what happens to us if you get caught?" she asked quietly.

"I'm not going to get caught."

"Do you know how many people have said that? And another thing, you don't even have anything to write on. Why would you put us…?"

The boy held up his finger, stuffed the pencil in his back pocket, and left the kitchen. A moment later he was back, unfolding a scrap of yellow legal-pad paper that was browning at the edges. He laid it on the table and placed the pencil on top of it. Silence descended on the room.

"This was Dad's," the boy said, his voice putting just a hair of emphasis on the man who would never return home. "They didn't find it; so after they came through, I hid it."

More silence, which seemed to hang in the air like a stench.

"What are you going to do with this stuff?" his mother said. "I know you wanted to be a blogger and some sort of social media superstar, but that was before the occupation. Why do you want to put yourself—us!—in such danger?"

After the occupiers had arrived, the Internet suddenly disappeared as if someone had flipped a great and terrible Off switch. One of the boy's neighbors, a hunched-over older gentleman named Earl, posited that the Internet and especially social media had been a scheme all along to divide and soften humanity. The occupiers had simply pulled the plug and cut the head off the snake.

That meant the boy's blog, *The Ancient Gallery*, had disappeared along with all of his social media accounts. Then came the Great Confiscation, when the occupiers—mostly real, sepia trench-coated troopers (not holos)—carrying large, smooth, ebony weapons, pulled up a white, unmarked semi on his street and went house to house. They loaded laptops, desktops, phones, televisions, cable boxes, and then reams upon reams of paper, legal pads, notepads, and every writing utensil they could find. Active resisters were immediately shot. The boy and his mother said nothing as they and their neighbors gaped at the troops from their living room windows. Vehicles were next.

Martial law was declared shortly thereafter, and residents all over Los Angeles and its sprawling suburbs were required to stay home between the hours of 6:00 p.m. and 7:00 a.m. And when they could emerge, they stood in serpentine lines for grain and yeast and the occasional vegetables, but no meat, which had been reserved for the fleshy peach-hued soldiers with slits for eyes and their officers. Holograms simply stood their ground on every street corner, ready to call in any infraction they had been programmed to perceive. And they had been programmed astutely.

"I need to write," the boy said to his mother, who displayed a disapproving frown. "At my heart, I am a writer, and I need to put pen to paper. There is no meaning here," he held up the paper, "unless *I* put it there."

"It doesn't matter what you want to do," came the dismissive response from the once-attractive woman he now felt sorry for.

"You're wrong."

"Am I? What are you going to write? A history of how miserable we are, which will only be found by the occupiers and burnt? It's a waste of time and a danger to you, me, and maybe this entire neighborhood."

"I know this scares you." He started making circles in the air with the pencil about an inch from the paper. "But I need to put something down on paper if not for anyone else but me. I have to feel alive again, some sense of the normal life we used to have."

And with that, he wrote for a very short while before refolding the paper and placing it in his shoe. *Maybe the safest place in the house*, he thought as he donned his black wool coat and stepped out into the late afternoon slate. It was 4:32 p.m.

He had people to talk to.

Present day

And he was lucid again, the ammonia inhalants doing their job, mining their way into his nostrils to the base of his brain before another blow to the head.

Black.

…then the cone-shaped light overhead…

"You know this to be true," said a voice in accented English. A real voice. Not the computerese vocal stylings of a hologram, which could pass as a foreigner on his first day of work. Canned commands and responses that were meant to be menacing, but in another time and place—preoccupation—would have been laughable.

Certainly, the blows were real. Fists. Rubber billy clubs. Rifle butts.

"Answer."

The boy didn't know what to say and couldn't form a coherent thought that had any chance to stop the rain. Christ and his crown of thorns had nothing on him.

"We have traced this to you," a blurry face said, the words a cacophony from on high, as a crisp photograph entered his blurred field of vision, the image of a forearm with an obviously homemade tattoo, its lines not crisp and clean, but rather frayed and fuzzy. The symbol was unmistakable.

A hashtag. #

"Never seen that before…"

"Of course not," the voice said. "This is the forearm of a woman from Las Vegas, Nevada. I doubt you have ever met her. I am concerned, however," he paused to take a hit off a cigarette, blowing the smoke in the boy's direction, "that the symbol it displays is a message that originated with you. Another example, please?"

The next photo showed the same ragged tattoo on what appeared to be a lower back, maybe where famous tramp stamps used to be found on women of questionable repute.

"This photograph is of a man from Bangor, Maine," the voice said. "Without doubt, you have never met him before, either."

More photos. More tattoos. Montezuma, Iowa. Bexar County somewhere in Texas. Dozens of them. And finally, a full-length photo of a resolute man from West Covina, California, with the same tattoo above his left breast.

Oh God. It's Uncle Rick.

"You will tell us how you achieved this," the voice said simply, "or there shall be unpleasant repercussions."

Once upon a time the bleary-eyed boy was a toddler and possessed the nickname Garbanzo as he pulled himself up onto the couch, while his mom and dad sang the song:

When the moon shines, my little Garbanzo

I'll be waiting for you at the kitchen door.

He'd laughed and laughed in those days. Garbanzo. A bean. It was just fun to say.

This boy was now a man.

"It's…it's," he barely could form the words.

"What?"

"It's…trending."

He didn't feel the bullet, but as he floated above the table, his blood and brains and sinew covering the photos, he could see more of them along the walls in the darkness.

Stacks and stacks.

Hundreds of them. Maybe thousands, all of the same things.

Body parts and tattoos.

Three years later

The crowd, thousands upon thousands—maybe even a million—filled the tree-lined landscape of Los Angeles' Grand Park. It was chilly, temperatures in the mid-fifties, but sunny at least with little wind coming off the ocean. For a February day, it was both balmy and relatively pleasant. And there was actual, genuine laughter that rippled across the masses as they stamped what remained of a light snowfall beneath their feet.

Laughter.

The dais was makeshift, no more than a church stage for children's plays, but it would do. After all, they weren't only there to see or hear the speaker, the democratically elected leader of New Los Angeles, one of dozens of newly renamed cities across the United States of America.

They were there to see the flagpole behind him.

The man, dressed in an aged, preoccupation charcoal suit and red tie, bore a resemblance to the old actor George Clooney. He carried at his side a white megaphone with red trim that stood out next to his dark clothing, perhaps the only mass communication device left after the occupiers had departed. Since there was no podium, he held up the megaphone and achieved an almost immediate, virtually absolute silence.

"Good afternoon," he said, the mechanically amplified words drifting over the heads of the many. "Today, we are here to celebrate our newfound freedom."

A thunder of applause went on for several minutes before the man held up the megaphone once again. "I don't need to tell you that many lives were lost in reclaiming our freedom, not only here but across our country," he said. "I often ask myself if it was worth it. Those people may have lived had we simply cowed to the whims of the occupiers.

"But what kind of life would they—would we—have had? I believe it was Zapata who said…," and at this those of Hispanic descent cheered, "it is better to die on your feet than live on your knees.' Well, I'm here to tell you that we are on our feet, and we are living. We…have…prevailed!"

Another round of applause that, this time, lasted at least three minutes.

"And now," the man said as the crowd simmered down, "and now we pay tribute to that unknown person, man or boy, woman or girl, lost to the mists of time and known but to God, who galvanized us and brought us to this place at this time."

He took off his suit coat, handed it to an attendant, and rolled up his sleeve. If you were close enough, you would have seen a symbol on the inside of his right forearm, just above his elbow. A hashtag. Like all the others, it was plain and black. He raised that arm to the sky as first the stars and stripes unfurled behind him.

Then a second flag—a plain yellow one with the same hashtag on the man's forearm—rose up behind it, resulting in more unabated applause.

"How many have this tattoo somewhere on your body?" he fairly yelled into the megaphone, and thousands of arms raised and swayed like the wave at a sporting event. "This was our rallying cry, our call to network and begin the only revolution that truly encompassed all of humanity.

"We don't know who you are," he went on, "but you are the reason for today. And your inspiration will be seen not only here, but throughout the world forever more."

As the applause gained speed once again and roiled to a new, unfathomable height, a woman deep within the bowels of the crowd sang to herself as tears traced down her cheeks.

"When the moon shines, my little Garbanzo, I'll be waiting for you at the kitchen door."

The Crash

Greeley, Colorado

The jetliner, a bone-white Airbus A320 with a fat blue logo, bounded over the neighborhood, wings waggling under the lemon sun. There was smoke, a lot of it, coming from the right-wing engine, and the dark contrail was an evil pencil mark crossing the cloudless mountain sky. Neighbors, alerted by a sudden cacophony, ran out onto their front porches and stared at death looming overhead. Children playing on front lawns dropped their balls and bikes and ran for the arms of their parents.

But Nick just stared at the inbound jet. He didn't move, even as the nose looked to bore directly into his eighty-pound frame.

"Nicky! Run!" Stacy screamed, like only a mother can, dropping her green dishtowel on the sidewalk parallel to tree-lined 4th Street, where she and her fifth-grader, her little boy, had lived since the divorce.

He just stood there, a half a block away, in apparent rapt curiosity that something like this could actually be happening. He loved airplanes, always had, and hoped to fly them one day. Maybe for the Colorado Air National Guard, which was based at the airport east of town. Sometimes he and his mother would drive over on a Saturday, have lunch at the

Barnstormer (he loved the French fries there), and watch the gray military C-130s take off and land.

There was a rumble and then a loud bang, and it appeared that the smoking engine was about to sever from the wing. The jet started to swerve to port just a hair and in the general direction of Nick's house, where his mother stood with her hand over her mouth. She took one or two steps backward.

That's when Nick lifted his arm, palm faced outward, and it stopped.

The jet, that is. It came to a complete halt just above a stately set of firs that surrounded Mr. and Mrs. Steele's corner property down the street. The smoke from the damaged engine suddenly pillared skyward, but the engine itself stayed in place, though it seemed to rock languidly like a baby in a cradle.

Stacy was wearing thin pink flip-flops, and she kicked both of them off as she tore up the street toward her son. Pebbles cut into her soles, but they felt like tiny pinpricks and then nothing at all. Her inclination was to scoop up her brave little man and shelter him from the onslaught of fire and burning shrapnel. They wouldn't survive, but at least he wouldn't die alone.

"Mom, wait!"

Stacy stopped, and that's when she felt the sharp stone embedded in her calloused heel.

But Nicky was speaking: "I can hold it, Mom!" Alternately stealing glances at her as he held his palm firm. "I can hold it. It's not moving. See?"

It just wasn't possible, but there it was. A jetliner in stasis in the sky. The right engine continued to sway as if it were being tapped by an unseen hand.

Was it a few minutes or an hour or more until she felt the hand on her shoulder? Stacy couldn't tell. She just shook it off in deference to her son, who hadn't moved at all. *His arm must be getting tired,* she thought.

"Miss Morgan," came an agitated, high-pitched voice behind her. Masculine. Stacy tried to escort the tonal pressure from her ears. The authorities would try to save at least her.

"Miss Morgan, you've got to come," he went on. "The Air Guard is here. C'mon! They want to talk to you."

Nicky seemed so…slight in this scene that felt like a disaster movie. She imagined black bars at the top and bottom of the screen and her son merely a tiny stick figure in the exact middle as the afternoon sky went dark with smoke and then white-hot with flames.

"I'm not leaving without my son," Stacy's gruff voice trailed off, and she began to lift her own arm inch by inch.

Then nothing for another undefined period of time before there was a new voice. Whereas the first was perhaps pushy, but ultimately harmless, this one was severe, commanding. No nonsense. It demanded attention and respect. Stacy turned.

The man was dressed in a dark-blue military uniform like the ones she and Nicky had seen many times at the airport. Not a local cop or county brownie. He was from the Air National Guard, and the black nameplate on his chest read "Schutz." Stacy didn't know anything about military rank, so she thought of him henceforth as Lurch. Because that's who he looked like, the walking corpse from *The Addams Family*.

"You need to come with me, now," he said. "My superiors need to consult with you."

"Again…not without my son."

Stacy was finally getting a little irritated with the fact that there were plenty of cops and military people walking around by now, but there was no game plan in place to save Nicky. She turned and looked back at her boy, who seemed to be squinting. The sun was just starting its westward descent, and there must have been a reflection from the plane's windshield. But his arm was still resolute.

Lurch lightly touched Stacy's elbow, and when she resisted, he grabbed it and started pulling her up the street. She struggled, but her neighbors paid her no mind, instead staring at the aircraft suspended in space and the little kid—what was his name, Nick?— who was apparently holding it there. Impossible. But there it was.

Lurch and Stacy reached a flurry of activity in front of a house three blocks away that she had driven by hundreds of times but never really stopped to admire. It was a quaint brownstone bungalow with flower boxes in front of the picture window and a wind chime hanging from a hook near the door. A little old lady she recognized as the owner, a widow, sat in a lawn chair with a cane over her lap. She looked like she wanted to move, to get the heck away from whatever was happening, but she was too infirm. Plus, what would all these soldiers do to her precious house?

It had become a command post of sorts, and Stacy tried to steal a glimpse of Nicky blocks away as Lurch pulled her up the porch steps into the house. She emerged in a living room, which abutted the dining room, where there was a large, long table. *Probably had seen many a wonderful Thanksgiving dinner,* Stacy thought as Lurch pulled out one of the chairs and forcibly sat her in it.

Staring back at her was a sullen, corpulent tub of a man with dark, curly hair and a dark, wavy moustache. His nameplate said "Tate," but Stacy could tell he was important due to the many gold trinkets on his uniform, including a set of wings above a rectangular field of multicolored ribbons.

"I'm General Ambrose Tate of the Colorado Air National Guard," he said. "We don't know what's going on out there," he waved his hand as if swatting a fly, "but we do know it's caused a stir at the highest levels of our government. The FAA and the United States Air Force will be here shortly. Meanwhile, I've been tasked with saving as many people on that plane as possible."

"What about my son?" Stacy fairly whispered.

Tate sat forward in his chair and tented his fingers as if this conversation was beneath him. "The mission priority here, from my superiors, is to save lives," he replied in a tone that reminded Stacy of her father, long dead but still somehow present. "Your son apparently has some sort of…*power*…we don't understand. But there is a window of opportunity here to save lives on both that aircraft and on the ground. We're going to seize that opportunity, and to do so, we need your help."

Stacy's only instinct, a motherly instinct, was to run. Run like hell up the street to her little boy, squeeze him like she did when he was a toddler, before he would say things like, "Aw, c'mon, Mom." She gripped her toes into the carpeting and then leapt. But she had temporarily forgotten Lurch lurking nearby, and he was too quick for her. His thick fingers bore into her shoulder as he sat her back down.

Silence, for about thirty seconds. Sirens outside. A decelerating jet engine further away. The pilots must have turned it….off? Was that the phrase?

Tate stood. "Miss Morgan, our strategy in this case is speed," he said. "We need to get the proper equipment in here quickly to get passengers off that aircraft. We also need to evacuate the area, which as you can already see is becoming a problem because of your son's, uh, *skill*."

Stacy thought about trying to run again, and thought better of it. Instead, she said, "It sounds like you've got this all planned out, *General*. Meanwhile, my kid is out there, holding everything together, and I've not heard one word—not one!—about how to help him!"

"My orders are…"

"Fuck your orders. What about my little boy?"

"Listen, we've got cranes coming in here from Denver and all over the God d…, er, place to get those people out. He's been holding his arm up for over two hours now."

Two hours? Stacy thought. *Really?*

"I need to know how long we have before your son's arm comes down," Tate hissed, placing two fat hands with hairy, stubby fingers on the dining room table. "I'm willing to bet if that arm comes down, everyone dies, maybe even you and me. I need to know if this has ever happened before. Anything you can tell me, anything at all, will be helpful."

Nicky was an average kid. Did well in school and was just starting to notice girls. Loved his grandparents and planes. Always planes. She remembered how excited he was about his first-ever plane trip, years earlier, to see his Uncle Peter in Tampa. *But most importantly,* Stacy thought, *he loves his mom and minds what I say.* He'd never given her any problems.

And as far as anything weird like what was going on outside, Stacy searched her memories. Nothing.

She had no idea how this was happening or how long Nicky could hold his arm in place while the rescuers worked.

"Why don't you just go over there and ask him?" Stacy said with a tone of disgust. "He's a smart kid. He'll tell you what you want to know."

A large vehicle turned up the streets and air hissed from its brakes.

"One of the cranes is here, General," Lurch said.

"Good, good," Tate said, doing what amounted to leaping into action for an obese man. "Get it into position on the port side and start getting those people off the plane."

Lurch barked orders at a subordinate, and the kid, probably just out of high school, dashed off.

"That crane out there," Tate pointed at the red monstrosity starting to trundle up the street, "is specially fitted with a basket to transport workers up and down tall buildings. There are 227 people on that plane, not including the pilots and flight attendants. Do you have any idea how long it will take to get everyone off? But we have to try. Even if we save one life, it'll be worth it."

"But why can't that life be my son's?" Stacy replied, tears now beginning to fill her eyes. "Isn't there something you can do? What if you get all those people off the plane? Then what?"

A pause.

"I don't know," Tate said. "I just don't know. We'll have to play it by ear. Right now, we have to focus on the task at hand."

A tear drifted from the corner of Stacy's right eye down her face and burned slightly. Her mouth was cotton, and she was starting to develop a headache.

"I want to see him," she said quietly.

"Out of the question, Miss Morgan."

"If he's going to die, I want to be with him. Besides," she said, lightening a little, "I could find out how long you might have."

Tate seemed to consider this line of thinking for several seconds. "This is Lieutenant Schutz," he finally said, motioning his chin toward Lurch. "He'll walk you to your son and then wait for a response to your question."

Stacy turned her head toward Lurch just in time to see his eyes widen just a hair. Probably not what he signed up for when he joined the Air National Guard.

"Lieutenant? Please escort Miss Morgan to her son," Tate said. "And may God be with you."

Lurch didn't say a word as he and Stacy walked up the street. A steady stream of neighbors, like refugees, were filing in the opposite direction, away from what was now being called Ground Zero by the cops and military people.

But it can't be Ground Zero yet, can it? Stacy thought. *There hasn't been a crash like 9/11 or whatever. No deaths,* although admittedly she didn't know what had happened, or what was happening, on the plane. The big red crane had eased past Nicky and was in place on his right side; its big folding arm with the basket was beginning the trek skyward. It looked like the basket could fit five, maybe six people.

It was going to be a long night. If Nickster could just hold on.

But then what?

Every step felt like one closer to oblivion. Stacy looked up at Lurch. There were the telltale signs of wetness along his temples. *Could be the late afternoon sun*, she thought. *Or could be the situation*. He probably had little kids at home somewhere in Greeley, a wife, maybe a dog or a cat or a parakeet. Somehow it comforted her to humanize this man a little. So different from her ex, who was short and smarmy. A player, a good-time Charlie always with a smug comment, but little substance. It ended after a few years, and she didn't have to fight hard for custody. He moved to Denver and saw Nicky maybe twice a year.

She wondered where he was right now, and if he knew all this had been started by their son. Rumor at the widow's house was that the TV stations were arriving and setting up. Maybe he was watching coverage on the tube.

Whatever. Not a thought priority.

There he was. Little Nicky Nicodemo. His arm was still pointed straight at the nose of the plane, but she noticed he was supporting all his weight on his right leg. That probably meant his arm was really, really sore. Stacy wondered if she could actually hold his arm to give him some relief, so she broke into a run. Lurch protested but, she was too quick for him and finally reached Nicky's side.

Her little boy was sweating, his taupe hair a tangled mess of knots, a U-shaped sweat mark on the front of his Colorado State T-shirt.

"H-hi, Mom," he said, alternately looking at the plane and then her. He smiled the sort of sad smile you see at funerals. "Am I doing it, right?"

"You sure are," Stacy said softly, and she came around to his right side and placed her hands on his protruded arm. There was heat, then sparks, and she hit the ground. The nose of the plane moved ever so slightly, maybe a foot or two, toward Nicky. The arm of the crane shook and the four people in it screamed. The damaged engine swung in a much more pronounced arc.

"Mom, you can't touch me, or the plane'll crash," Nick said, this time not even looking at her. "This is something I have to do on my own. You can't help me."

Another pause in a day filled with them.

"But can you do it?" Stacy said, gathering herself up with Lurch's help. "Can you hold it until all these people are off? She regretted saying "all those people," because it made it feel like there was a long, long way to go, and that might be bad psychologically for her big guy.

"I'm going to have to," he said. "I just have to. Those people need me to. I can't let them die."

"Son, my name is Lieutenant Schutz," Lurch broke in. "You're very brave, do you know that? If you can hold your arm up until all those people are off the plane, I'll make sure you get to take a flight on an actual fighter jet."

"Really? Seriously?"

It's a smart ploy, Stacy thought. Took Nick's mind off his arm and probably gave him some relief.

"No fooling, son," Lurch said. "They've got Raptors out at the base. Do you know what they are?"

"Yes sir, the F-22," Nicky said. "I've seen them out at the airport. You can get me on a Raptor?"

Stacy doubted that. I mean, he's just a little kid. They probably didn't even have a helmet his size. But she rolled with it. It was keeping him alive, and that was her first priority.

"Sure," Lurch said. "Can you promise me you'll hold your arm up until all those people are off the plane?"

"How long will that take?"

Suddenly, Stacy didn't like where this was going.

"Awhile, son," Lurch said. "Maybe all night. Do you think you can do that?"

Nicky wriggled his nose a little.

"You're scaring him," Stacy broke in. "Leave him alone!"

"Ma'am, I have my orders," Lurch said plainly.

"I can't believe…"

"Mom, I can do it," Nick said. "But can you stay with me? Please?"

Stacy turned to Lurch, who now looked like he wanted nothing more than to get the hell out of there and back to not only the widow's house, but his normal life, maybe a quaint three-bedroom in the Glenmere/Cranford neighborhood. He hesitated and then said, "Okay."

Lurch didn't sprint up the street, but it was a kind of walking/running mix that made him look like he was on his way to the bathroom.

Stacy sat cross-legged on the pavement and marveled at the courage of her little boy as the sun finally dipped beyond Mr. and Mrs. Steele's firs and evening encroached. They didn't talk much, instead watching the crane take five minutes to lift, another five minutes to load and then another five minutes to lower, the only sound a buzzing drone interrupted by brake hisses. It was excruciating, and as evening became night, the feds had arrived and had sent in soldiers to set up big lights on either side of her and Nick. They illuminated the terrified faces of passengers on the jet whose lives had been saved by this little boy they didn't even know.

"Mom, what did you think I'd grow up to be?" Nick said at about 11:30 p.m.

"Well," Stacy said, "A pilot, I guess. But when you were a little snug, I thought you'd grow up to be a fireman or policeman."

And then she stopped. He was speaking in a forlorn tone and in the past tense, as if he were resigning himself to something.

"Mom, my arm really hurts," he said. "I don't know how long much longer I can hold it."

A nearby soldier, another post-high school kid, took a few steps backward and then *ran*—not walked—to what looked to be his officer. The officer looked at him, then Nick, then Stacy, and spoke into a microphone in an animated fashion.

Not good, Stacy thought. *Not good.*

"Mom?"

"I'm here, baby, I'm here," Stacy said.

The officer ran up to them. "We've got almost everybody off the plane," he said. "Can you hang on for a little while longer?"

"I don't think I can…" Nicky's voice trailed off.

"You have to, young man. You have to. We're so close, and we've saved so many."

Nick's arm dropped an inch, two inches, three. The nose of the aircraft jiggled a little, and the wing dipped toward the ground, causing the door opening on the left side of the plane to point nearly skyward and away from the crane's basket. Anyone who wanted to escape now would have to climb up and out of the doorway.

"Shit!" the officer yelped. "Come on, people, move! This bird's coming down. Get that basket in place. How many we got yet?"

A voice from behind him squawked, "About two dozen, sir!"

"Get 'em out of there *now!*"

For the next thirty or so minutes, Stacy watched little heads pop out of the doorway and then their bodies climb into the basket. They were taking bigger loads of people, probably unsafe loads, as many as eight or nine, she couldn't tell with the shadows.

Nicky's arm was shaking now, the fingers of his little hand curled downward. The sweat stain had long enveloped his shirt and he was alternating his weight between both legs with alarming frequency.

The end was at hand.

Maybe the plane won't blow up, Stacy thought. Maybe it will just hit the ground and just…sit there.

Doubtful.

"Mommy?"

"Yes, baby."

"I love you."

"I love you, too." Then, "Are you okay?"

"I can't do it anymore, Mommy. I'm so tired, and my arm hurts."

"Last one!" came a voice from somewhere within the hot lights. "Pilots are next!"

Something leapt within Stacy. She got to her feet and got as close to Nicky as she dared. Didn't want to get zapped again, but there was a warmth between a mother and son that was palpable now.

"You've got this, baby," she said. "See? They're taking the pilots out now. And after that…"

"Then what?" Nicky replied. "They can't save me, Mommy. You can't save me. You have go to too."

The crane was in its final descent, and Stacy could see the desperate looks on the faces of two pilots and four flight attendants, three older women and one younger man. So close to salvation and yet so far. Even they could tell that Nicky was losing resolve.

The officer suddenly appeared. "Ma'am, you've got to come with us," he said, "everyone's out. They're calling for you."

"Not without my son."

"Ma'am, please, you have to come, I have my orders."

"No!"

The next few moments didn't exist for Stacy. There were the lights and Nicky's terrified face, then there was darkness and finally light again. Her arms were held securely by muscular hands that wouldn't let go.

"Nooooo!"

Then she was in the back of a truck and heard the finality of a clicking lock. She pounded the doors and window, screamed some more, and then fell to the floor and curled up in the fetal position.

A loud bang outside and a movie-worthy explosion. The truck rocked back and forth before coming to a complete stop.

"My baby," Stacy whimpered. "Oh, my baby, my little Nicky Nicodemo."

Did she pass out? Must have.

"Holy hell!" came from outside somewhere.

The door flew open and there was Lurch, who was actually smiling and pointing up the street to a little stick figure emerging from the flames.

Not on fire, mind you. Just walking, his right arm against his side and a satisfied smile on his face.

Was he real? Or was she filling in a tragic hole with a hologram?

Stacy's first inclination was to run—run as fast as she ever had, scoop up her little boy, and never let him go, to both protect him from the flames licking the pitch sky and nurture him in some way. But her cerebral cortex couldn't send the command to her arms and legs to move, because it just wasn't sure he was alive. She was utterly inert, and so she simply watched in stunned silence as Nicky approached with pep in his step and hair that was sweaty and mussed.

Finally, she managed to stumble down the truck's one step and hit her knee on the ground, resulting in a bloody scrape. She resisted the urge to curse, and suddenly he was there, her Nicky. His hand was cool, his palms and fingers smooth.

Somehow, he had survived.

"Did you see, Mom? Did you see?" Nick said, trying to help Stacy to her feet. Instead, she knelt down on her scraped knee. It stung, but she ushered that thought from her mind.

"Yeah, baby, I saw it," Stacy said, which wasn't entirely true, of course, but she rolled with it.

"Did I do good?"

"You were fantastic."

Then Nicky stopped and looked at Lurch, who actually looked as if he had moist eyes. *Very unmilitary*, Stacy thought, but she smiled gratefully anyway.

"When can I get that ride in the Raptor?" Nick said.

THE GREATER GOOD

Twenty minutes later, Spencer's heart was still racing. Taylor was becoming more adventurous in her old age, if you consider the "big 3-0" old. Maybe she was getting something out of all that porn he implored her to watch with him, cajoling her reluctance with promises of anything that she happened to want at the time. He did have a track record of following through, although it usually took three or four sullen reminders. Like many of his financially unsophisticated clients, Taylor was a jughead. Comical simpletons with big dreams, unaware of the stark reality behind their stout walls.

At thirty-six, Spencer was getting up in age himself, and sure, he had the dream: a sculpted bod, plenty of Scotch, the high-rise Gold Coast apartment overlooking Lake Michigan, the pitch-as-night Porsche in the garage downstairs, even a valet and a doorman. No use in listing it all here; suffice to say it was all the spoils that come with the ability to talk anyone into doing just about anything like Taylor could. Like his jughead clients, who didn't know a sound investment from the holes in their asses. Investment banking was the shit, no doubt. Legalized robbery for those who had the balls to push the limits. And Spencer had more than balls. He had conviction.

But a piece was missing. Taylor was Taylor—she was easy. It wasn't a challenge anymore. She was the fallback position after hedging a substantial bet on another babe that would ultimately fall through time and time again. Taylor was reliable, let's say. He wasn't in love with her; hell, he wasn't even in lust with her like he had been when she was twenty-six and just starting at the firm. Was that really four years ago? Had she really been one of his conquests? Hard to believe. Hard to remember. But there was something more out there.

Ashley. She was fresh out of school. *Ohio State?* Spencer thought. *One of the Big Ten, anyway.* Educated, but not in the ways of the world, just how he liked 'em. Young, dumb, and full of cum. T&A in tight skirt and fuck-me pumps. The look he slid in her direction as he gathered up his shit after the daily roundup meeting was returned in full force; he had made his presence *known.*

But there was the telltale sign of a demure coyness, a come-hither sexuality that danced around in his mind when he was back home doing Taylor, who fancied herself Miss Suzy Homemaker. Hey, at least she picked up his dry cleaning.

He was a prick, and he realized it. So was his dad, and he was on his yacht, sailing around the world with some bimbo he met in the Greek isles. "Mom." *Right.* Life was about calculation as much as conviction. Everything was something to possess or get rid of.

Upon the summer breeze drifted the sounds of traffic below on Lake Shore Drive, a consistent humming that almost seemed interwoven with the rhythm of Spencer's heart, which had slowed considerably as he contemplated the state of his life.

There was a crack in the plaster in the far right corner that snaked about two feet into the room; better have Taylor call maintenance to have that patched. Meeting with a new client tomorrow, likely another jughead. Gotta get out the dog-and-pony show. Maybe Ashley would help him get ready. Probably. He had influence, perhaps even divine, over her.

And then he was drifting alone along the leading edge of verisimilitude.

***

Blackness to slate brush strokes overhead to a rusty-brown texture under his fingernails. It was the trench again, the damned, stinking trench; inches of water covered his boots as he rested his backside on a makeshift ledge of earth and sandbags. The collar of his tunic pinched his neck, and he pulled it with his right index finger. Salutes of faceless men slogging by in saucepan helmets and leg puttees disturbed the muck and mud of the trench. The scream of a shell overhead exploded well behind him, and then the rat-a-tat-tat of machine gun fire.

The men didn't even flinch. *But they look afraid,* he thought.

And me? *I am not afraid.*

No, I am not.

Yea, though I walk through the valley of the shadow of death I will fear no evil.

For thou art with me; thy rod and thy staff, they comfort me. (Psalm 23)

Just like Clementine's latest letter, folded away squarely and neatly in the front pocket of his tunic, over his heart. Maybe it would ward off the Gerrys' bullets if they decided to make a push this morning deep into the heart of the Western Front. All indicators, including those from pilots of aeroplanes high above, were that the Germans, probably as exhausted as his own men, were amassing in their own trenches hundreds of yards across No Man's Land.

"Major?" came a voice from nearby. He looked up.

"Major, sir, a communiqué just arrived for you," said Corporal Stansbury, his de facto aide-de-camp. "It's from HQ. They are requesting an immediate response."

The major liked Stansbury. Son of a Derbyshire farmer. Salt-of-the-earth sort of blighter who would win this war. He had that conviction deep within the fabric of his soul. *This terrible conflict can't go on forever*, he surmised many times in his fresh weeks at the front, and men like Stansbury, by virtue of their very presence, eased his mind.

"Sir?" Stansbury said, rubbing his hands along the sides of his trousers for warmth.

The major smiled just a bit and opened the communiqué. It was a missive from Colonel Berkeley to return to headquarters about a mile behind the line, where he was waiting with the French General Proulx to discuss defense arrangements in event the Germans did, indeed, advance. Since an attack was likely imminent, perhaps within the hour, it behooved him to hurry.

"I'll be off now, Corporal," the major said, picking himself up from the makeshift ledge and reaching for his sidearm for probably the twentieth time that day. He adjusted his own saucepan and gave one final order. "Stay here and mind the store," he said with a growing grin and grabbed his peak cap, which was necessary for any meeting with a general, British or otherwise. He was fastidious with maintaining military order with rank-and-file troops, but was thankful he could allow his personality to shine somewhat with Stansbury, who seemed to appreciate it as well.

Stooping low, he began the trek down the trench toward the interchange that would lead to the rear. He had just about reached it when the familiar whistle of an incoming shell caused him to spin around and duck for cover. The explosion, when it came, was so close he wondered if the time had finally come to meet his maker.

Yea, though I walk through the valley of the shadow of death…

After the concussion had subsided, he shook his head, clumps of dirt dripping off of his helmet like black raindrops. He peered toward his safe place, where Stansbury should have been crouched low amongst the sandbags.

Instead, the young corporal had been disemboweled, his torso connected to his pelvic region only by the torn fabric of his tunic, his cap still sitting jauntily on his head. From where the major stood, he could see the young man's eyes affixed on the gray sky above, almost looking surprised that he had been hit. A fine pink mist filled the air, and a growing pool of blood now mixed with the trench's muddy water.

Stansbury. Oh God.

***

The cry echoed as if a door had suddenly been slammed shut. Spencer sat up so fast he had a head rush, and he had to wait a moment for the rest of the shadow-wrapped room to fill his field of vision. He touched his pectorals to make sure he was really there back in the apartment. His breathing came in short gasps, and his mouth was filled with a sour-tasting saliva.

"Babe?" Taylor.

"Go back to sleep," Spencer replied with more of a growl than he intended, throwing his legs over the side of the bed. He was still naked and tried to find his boxers with his right foot.

"It was that same dream again, wasn't it?" Taylor asked as she sat up in the light-blue satin chemise she had gotten especially for last night.

"Will you just let it go?" Spencer now barked, then softened. "It was a nightmare. Just a nightmare."

God, Taylor can be such a pain in the ass.

"Okay, sorry," she said, pulling up the comforter and rolling over.

"All right, all right," he said, climbing on the bed and pulling at the comforter. "Yeah, it was the same dream. I was in the trench, and this time, another soldier got killed by bomb just a few seconds after I had walked away."

Taylor sat up again. "What are you going to do about these dreams?" she said, grabbing both of his hands with a pleading look on her face. "Babe, I get that work is stressing you out, but this can't go on. You've got to find out why you're dreaming about World War I. World War I! You don't even like history. This just isn't normal."

Spencer had considered seeing a therapist, but decided against it. That would have been a sign of weakness he couldn't afford. But the dreams, which had started with him merely walking through the trench past soldiers with their backs turned to him, had grown exponentially more vivid in recent weeks, particularly from the auditory and sensory points of view. Tonight's was the first time he had seen someone killed, and perhaps for the first time in his life, Spencer was the slightest bit unsettled. Maybe it was time to revisit that whole therapy thing, privately, of course, but that bridged to another thought.

What if it were really true? That if you die in your dream, you were really dead.

"Bullshit," he murmured to himself as he pulled on his boxers. He was a bull like his dad. A hustler, an irresistible force in business and in life.

But Taylor was wise in her own way, and while it was hard for him to admit it, but maybe she was right. Maybe the time had come to get to the bottom of whatever his nightmares meant and why they were happening. Maybe a circuit breaker in his brain had been tripped and just needed to be reset. Personally, Spencer thought psychology was mostly hokum, a land occupied by nonanalytical hippie wannabes (or has-beens) who couldn't make it in the real world of business, where the all-important economy was grown and nurtured by people like him.

There had to be resolution, though, and putting the problem through the lens of business, he needed a strategy in place to achieve the objective. To do that, he needed a strategist, which is why he found himself the following week sitting in a cozy, unobtrusive office across from Dr. Shelley Patzner, LCSW. Spencer hadn't done any real research—he was far too busy for that—so he'd selected an in-network therapist from his company's medical plan, a female, of course, and one who had a hot name. Shelley. Reminded him of a booty call he had had at U of I. *Hmm. Wonder whatever happened to her.*

But Dr. Patzner wasn't what he expected. She was only five feet tall with long black hair that featured copious streaks of gray, tortoise-shell glasses with dark frames that made her face seem smaller than it actually was, and a frumpy sweater and skirt that made her look like a school marm. She had a weak, limp-wristed handshake that Spencer immediately didn't trust. He rolled his eyes when she noted in her intro that she was a facilitator of her patients' well-being: mind, body and soul. *Hippie.*

"What brings you here, Spencer?" she said after settling into her wingback armchair that didn't look very comfortable.

Spencer threw his right arm over the back of the couch and crossed his left leg, giving her a front-row seat to his crotch. Hell, may as well give the old girl a thrill, considering he didn't plan to return. Dr. Patzner didn't blink.

"There are these dreams," he began and then proceeded to give her the basic highlights. He was an officer in the British Army during World War I, stationed in the trenches somewhere on the Western Front. Geography and history weren't his strong suits. They'd started a few weeks ago and were benign at first, more flashes of men wearing brown helmets and uniforms and speaking in heavily accented English he could barely understand.

"And then, about a week ago, I had a really intense dream where a soldier got killed, but the funny part was, the bomb—or was it a shell? I don't know—went off a few seconds after I had left this bunker area and someone died," he said. "So what do you think, Doc? Am I going crazy?"

He said that last part with just a pinch of a smile, wholly designed to shroud any perception of nerves that might show through. Orchestrate that perception of toughness.

Dr. Patzner considered this with pursed lips for more than thirty seconds. "Tell me, Spencer," she began, "what do *you* think these dreams represent?"

For Spencer, being caught off guard was like standing in the middle of an ominous forest at dusk. Better move fast or the bogeyman will get you.

"How should I know?" he said. "That's why I'm here."

"No need to get defensive," Dr. Patzner said firmly. "I'm only asking because it's best to get the opinion of the client first and then build from there. In my experience, they often have the answer; they simply need to articulate it. So again I ask you, what do you think these dreams represent?"

With a condescending shake of his head, Spencer decided to play the good doctor's game.

"They represent…my conflicted feelings about my insane ability to bed as many women as humanly possible." A slight chuckle.

No hesitation from the good doctor. "And I think they have to do with your fear of vulnerability," she said. "Often, dreams about war have to do with some hidden turmoil in a person's life. I speculate you fear being in a position in which you could die. Isn't that right, Spencer? Search your feelings. I suspect you already know this."

Silence. Heavy, deafening silence.

"Vulnerability?" Spencer finally said, voice raising an octave. He was back in the woods.

"Yes, vulnerability. I think if you…"

"Listen, lady, I'm vulnerable to *nothing*. I've got the perfect life because I busted my ass to get to where I am." Which wasn't exactly true; it was because of Dad's money, but he rolled with it. "And anything you say that challenges my manhood ain't gonna fly. If anything, I'm *in*vulnerable, especially to feelings I don't wanna have. I'm bulletproof."

Dr. Patzner sighed and sat up in her chair. "Don't forget, Spencer," she said quietly and matter-of-factly, "you came to me. I can help you if you'll let me. Let's work this out. Trust me, you'll feel a whole lot better and chances are the dreams will go away. Let me help."

It was 5:34 p.m., exactly 120 minutes after his session. Spencer had just destroyed a can of Pringles and a couple of beers when Taylor came over. Ten minutes after that, the sex was aggressive, so much so that Taylor had to tell him to slow down and then, "Stop! You're hurting me."

There was no remorse per se in Spencer. The closest he came to that sentiment was actually stopping, rolling over on his back, and expecting her to mount him.

Instead, she pulled what Taylor always pulled. "How did it go at the therapist?" she said, kneeling on her side of the bed, scratching an itch on her big toe. Stupidly, he had let news of his appointment with Dr. Patzner slip.

"What? We're back to that? She told me I was perfect, no problems mentally. I'm not headed to the funny farm."

"Why am I not believing this?"

He just shook his head and rolled his eyes. *Typical Taylor.*

"Testy, testy," she said, placing her hands on her knees, her French-manicured hands dainty in the late-afternoon sunlight surging through the blinds. "You want to know what I think? I think the therapist found something, and you're not willing to admit it."

Spencer cocked his head in her direction and his lower jaw dropped about an inch. Any arousal he had felt had disappeared up the chimney of his mind. Insolence!

He stood, his penis now flaccid. That seemed to create a sense of unease in Taylor as she sat back on her legs and straightened that same blue chemise. She started to speak, then thought better of it, but changed her mind. "Spencer, I just want you to confide in me. That's going to be my job—our job—when we get married. If we can't talk to each other, if we can't confide in each other when times are tough, where does that leave us?"

He paused, turned toward the pistachio-velvet slipper chair in the corner Taylor had picked out— like a lot of things in the apartment—grabbed her smart black pants suit and white blouse with one muscular hand, and tossed it in her direction.

Sleep drifted on Spencer that night like the clouds outside that slowly made their way across Chicago toward Lake Michigan. Taylor wasn't a consideration; she'd be back. That's why she wasn't a challenge. He didn't have to chase her down and make any heartfelt apologies or any stupid promises to be better, do better, or try harder. She was probably with her folks in La Grange tonight or maybe with a girlfriend. Maybe he'd call her tomorrow, maybe he wouldn't. But either way, she would be back at his door within a couple of days like the lap dog she always was, probably apologizing for pushing him too hard. Jughead.

Sleep was a figment of his imagination that night.

***

Strangely, the bullets being expelled from the Vickers toward the abyss of No Man's Land made no sound, just a steady, heavy thrum in his mind. He watched the belted bullets enter the firing chamber one by one with the empty belt emerging like a dead snake. The scent of gunpowder settled in his nostrils, finding a place among the body odor and abandoned rotting soup.

They were coming: dark-clad figures in the early morning haze that looked more like ghosts floating over the landscape pockmarked by preattack artillery. His men were already firing their Enfields into the abyss, reloading, and firing again and again, but the still the ghosts kept coming. The staccato shouts of German drifted distantly over the barbed-wire reinforcements toward the trench, which was a terror unto itself.

Men were going to die now. His men. Perhaps even he himself. The letter to Clementine was still folded in his upper right breast pocket over his heart.

How does one prepare for death on the battlefield? For a professional soldier like the major, was it everlasting contemplation of an inevitable end? Or, more likely for an enlisted man, is it a process that occurs in the space of seconds?

The Lord is my shepherd.

The Lord is my shepherd; I shall not want. Psalm 23:1

The throat of the private feeding the Vickers seemed to explode with a sound like chopping wood, careening him into the back wall of the trench, the helmet falling over his face and then into the water on the floor, revealing his cold blue eyes. Like Stansbury's, they were open, and he even seemed to have a slight smile on his face, a naïve smile like a mischievous little boy.

The major grimaced and stepped over the private, Walcott was his name, he believed, a youngster from Manchester or Liverpool or one of the northern cities. Parents were shopkeepers. He had heard him talk about it when he arrived at the front line just after Stansbury had been killed. Poor blighter. If only the ravages of war didn't douse flaming youth.

He grabbed the belt with one hand and kept the feed going, while gripping his sidearm. The helmeted Germans were inching closer, screams of *Attacke!* And *Nein, nein!* and *Scheisse!* growing louder and counteracting the cackle of the Vickers.

The first ghosts that emerged from the haze and ventured within yards of the trench were cut down by the Vickers, their bodies simply dropping as if their drawers were suddenly filled with lead. But their comrades were legion and swarmed behind them, a tried-and-true strategy to overwhelm a section of the enemy's line with force in order to punch through, perhaps all the way to Paris. Or even (shudder) London. Was that possible? He permitted a brief, terrifying thought of Clementine, warm and safe at Cromwell Road, with Gerry guards stationed outside, a zeppelin overhead.

The *Stahlhelm*-covered German who leapt into the trench to his left was a professional soldier, without doubt. No shouts, no words even, just a countenance of steely determination as he attended to his task. *Gott strafe England.* He had been indoctrinated to kill the British.

The major raised his sidearm, and the recoil of the weapon forced the barrel into the air, the scent of gunpowder spitting into the wind, which now featured a cold mist. His attacker stumbled backward; the bullet had entered his body at the point where the sternum and rib cage come together. Still, in a very German way, he maintained his air of steely resolve and attempted to pick up his bayoneted rifle that had fallen into the trench water. As he reached and reached for the rifle, he landed on his backside with a splash, the blood pooling in the middle of his chest.

The major shot him again, this time in the area of the heart, as the scream of an incoming shell overhead pierced the chaos down below. The German flailed backward and moved no more. The major simply stared at him, as his surroundings darkened and then faded completely to black.

***

Spencer was awake again as if he were now finally getting used to these illusions, though he had never killed in them before. The killing didn't really bother him. In fact, it was actually a relief in certain respects: if confronted by another man whose intention was to kill, he would have the temerity to return the favor, albeit subconsciously. If he actually faced this threat on the streets of Chicago, there was no doubt he could put another man down. For good, if necessary.

The morning passed like every other one for Spencer, and the fact that he and Taylor were apparently on the outs was a minor irritation, if anything at all. Sure, she'd be back. That was Taylor, old reliable. The default position. But in the meantime…in the meantime, he had other things to do.

Spencer's father had an impressive sexual résumé—from what he knew, and he knew a lot—but they had one thing in common: top-heavy blondes. That bimbo in his tub with him somewhere in the Mediterranean fit that description. *What was her name again? Sofia?* His dad had texted him a photo of her in a shapely red bathing suit, reminiscent of *Baywatch*, her blonde curls lilting over her shoulders.

Not bad, Pops. You still got it. That offhandedly reminded him to call his mother, who was single and depressed in Connecticut.

He made a point of liberally scanning Ashley across the oak conference room table and fantasized about her in that same red suit, her own straight, blonde hair waterfalling behind her as she lounged next to a pool somewhere, maybe Vegas or Miami. She looked up and smiled at him devilishly, as if she could read his mind, as she tapped her tablet with perfectly manicured nails after a conference call with their new out-of-state jughead. *She's primed*, he thought. *Now it's time to turn over the engine.*

The invitation for drinks after work was unrehearsed—a kind of, hey, let's loosen up a little as we rehash that conference call, and isn't this new client a total fool? After two or three drinks, what the hell, may as well have dinner at Gibson's. He couldn't have cared less about Ashley's background, about growing up in Rockford's Machesney Park, her Penn State education—that was it, not Ohio State—the virtues of Instagram, her pug, Mangia, and how she really wanted to make a difference in the world. Blah, blah, blah. Typical millennial bullshit, and he got bored quickly. But there was that ass, that perfect, marble-round specimen that evolved into stick-like legs supported by four-inch, red patent leather pumps.

Getting to the sexual component of the evening wasn't much of a challenge, either; she told him she had been waiting for his entrée for awhile now, and he had to admit that he regretted not making his move sooner. (*Dammit, Taylor. Get out of my mind!*) Her body was as curved and smooth and creamy as he had imagined it would be, while her hands touched every relevant part of his until they were united in passion, a singular form in the fabric of time and place.

***

But occupying that same time and place was the major, who—despite Clementine's missives to be sensible and "take the trenches in small doses"—had heard the weak, feeble cries in English almost as soon as the Germans had retreated to their own line. He stepped delicately over the German he had killed, out of respect for a fellow professional soldier, to seize a handheld periscope. Peeing over the trench, he spied a saucepan and to its right was a helmetless Private Hubbard, an original member of the Queen's Own Oxfordshire Hussars from '14. Volunteer, but like them all, a good, solid Tommy. Worth risking his own life for.

The major handed off the periscope and pulled himself up over the top and into No Man's Land, the acrid smoke lilting over the desolate, rolling landscape. His heartbeat thundered in his ear in perfect rhythm with Spencer's 100 years in the future as he approached climax with Ashley's legs wrapped around his back, pulling him even further inward.

Her screams of ecstasy mingled with Private Hubbard's cries of terror as the major slid like a tackling footballer and grabbed his shoulders. There was a wound about a foot in circumference where the major could see his off-white innards, probably intestines. Spurting blood. The private's hands were shaking, his brown hair matted.

The German seemed to pop up five feet away from a small berm created by shellfire, aimed his rifle squarely at the major, and fired—the flash an electric star. He'd probably spent much of his life hunting boar in the Ruhr Valley, perhaps, or in the woods well north of Munchen. The soldier was well acquainted with prey, and he simply could not miss.

The major's chin jutted and his body tensed, expecting certain penetration and the bliss that would undoubtedly come from crossing over into eternity.

Ashley's cooing as her hands ran across his chest. The first wound appeared above his right nipple. A scream, this time in terror.

The German frowned, reloaded, and fired again and then a third time.

The major simply remained in the muck, pushing himself with his heels as he carried along Private Hubbard, who was now moaning.

"M-Major," Hubbard quavered, "Major Churchill…"

A second wound appeared on Spencer's stomach, spurting blood onto Ashley's naval, and then a third in the middle of his forehead. He lurched backward and fell over the upholstered cedar chest, something else Taylor had picked out. His eyes, like his mouth, were slightly open.

Seemingly endless agony that echoed across a century.

Decades later, as he regaled his war cabinet with tales of his Great War misadventures, the prime minister remarked he could have sworn he heard a woman's scream at the moment that third bullet was fired.

THE DANCE OF THE SHADOWS

Fish Creek, Wisconsin

Their shadows are dancing on the wall again tonight. They're grayed-out silhouettes of his feathered hair and thin legs, her ample breasts and curves. His hands begin their slow ride down her hips, while her fingers lock behind his neck. He twirls her away from him, grabbing her hand at the last moment, the moment of truth, before violently pulling her back into his embrace.

Their lips meet. And the dance starts all over again.

I can see their reflection in my ashtray, the filterless Pall Mall smoke drifting languidly toward the jaundiced light over the kitchen sink that births them every night. They're alive, and I wonder if I am. If I've ever been since it all went down.

Did I die that night or something inside of me?

Did I die so they could live on this way?

She is a girl I never knew. He is Chase, and God do I miss him.

The phone rings, and I'm back in my room in Fish Creek, Door County, Wisconsin, U.S. of A. It's early evening and I've returned from the University of Wisconsin. I'm a crazy woman, calling his house every hour on the hour. "No, Chase isn't here," his dad says for the third time. "But don't worry, I'll have him call you as soon as he gets back. He's around somewhere."

The whole point of a surprise is to spring it on someone, particularly *that* someone, and I sense the momentum ebbing. The streetlight outside my bedroom window is starting to create static shapes on the walls: straight lines and circles and even half an octagon from a pile of my new textbooks on the desk.

I'm a lily-white college freshman, naïve. He's entering his senior year at Gibraltar High. We had broke up seventy-two hours earlier, before Pa piled me and all of my belongings into the minivan and drove me the four hours south to Madison for college.

"It's for the best," Chase had said. You're gonna meet a guy there, you know you will. I don't want to hold you back. You're too special for that, a diamond in the sky, the tallest rose in the garden. Experience what the big world beyond Door County has to offer. You'll be fine," he said. "So will I."

I stewed for a few days and then in desperation that Friday afternoon, September 1, 2000, I connected with some fat dude named Bumpers (license plate BUMPRS) and hitched a ride back to Fish Creek. He hit on me the entire way, even telling me I have nice boobs and butt, but I'm not having any of it.

Chase. The surprise is for him. I'm home.

I want him. Still.

Like I said, I'm a crazy woman on the phone when I get home, the sun setting beyond the thousandfold maples and beeches that make up Peninsula State Park. I can't see the seventy-five-foot Eagle Tower from my bedroom, a behemoth of 108 steps, where Chase and I first kissed that June, but I know it's out there.

I feel like that's where he is. I sense it.

Is he alone?

My heart takes a swim in my gut.

Pa's out with the minivan, so I'm pedaling my ancient twelve-speed up Shore Road, past the golf course with a party apparently going on in the clubhouse; light laughter drifted over greens and bunkers. There's a bright crescent moon overhead that illuminates the road for me, and we're back to stilling shadows. A few cars pass on the left side, then one close enough on the right that I have to dart onto the gravel, the wheels crunching under my Birkenstocks. *Bastard.*

Eagle Tower's silhouette comes into view on the right as I head up the hill, pumping and pumping. It's like a soldier standing at attention, the angles of the three platforms perfectly straight, the tucked-away steps zigzagging underneath, and the oaken posts turned slightly inward. I've been there, I don't know, maybe 1,000 times before, but never in the tizzy I'm in now. I always go there to contemplate. I don't have a Zen place, but if I did, it would be Eagle Tower.

I skid my bike to a stop on the gravel next to the stone wall that half-rings the tower and lean against cold boulders that were fashioned by earnest and poor Civilian Conservation Corps (CCC) men back in the 1930s. *The whole is greater than the sum of its parts*, I think as I run my hand across the smooth surface, kicking off my left sandal and stretching out my sore foot.

A giggle. And another, this time a male voice. His voice. From somewhere high above, but out of my field of vision. Blocked by the tower's posts and platforms.

I find my sandal, briskly walk to the opposite side, and look up to see a silhouette, easily ten feet away from the uppermost platform, above the trees. Clearly two people locked in an embrace, but actually levitating like those Buddhist monks you see on YouTube or Nat Geo.

Yeah, you heard me right. Levitating. Just floating there in the darkness. I can't say it any plainer than that.

"What the hell…?" I recall whispering into the pitch, my hollow words bouncing off of the stone wall and spilling onto the gravel.

People talk about how they remember when they first heard about 9/11 or the space shuttle explosion or even Pearl Harbor from way back when. That moment was my 9/11. I remember every last detail of it. I remember that my nipples were hard because it was chilly, and there was a funny tingling in my spine as I stared skyward.

I can still see his arms spread-eagle like Christ on the cross and her arms around his neck as if she were ready to kiss him.

From my viewpoint, it almost looked as if they were….dancing in the sky.

An impossibility. And yet…

"Hey!" Even in the encroaching darkness, I can still see two heads turn, their arms folding inward. "Hey! Chase!"

They're holding each other as they hit the ground with an earthquake-like crack, separating only when they each bounce about ten feet in the air.

My heart splashes into my stomach, and the responsibility for what I've done reverberates up my spine and into my cerebral cortex.

The key message: You've done a bad, bad thing.

Oh God. Oh God.

But there is no God who saves, not tonight anyway.

I don't even feel myself running toward them. It's as if I'm paralyzed below my waist, but my head feels the sensation of moving because the night wind is burning my cheeks.

I can't even bear to look at them. But I must.

The tears, they flow, of course. The liquid is hot and burns my face more than the wind. Somehow

I realize I don't know her. She's not somebody from Gibraltar High. Maybe Sevastopol or Southern Door? But I cry for her. And I cry for Chase, who's gone, too.

Admittedly, my first love. And, as of this writing, perhaps my last; I don't know.

The rest of the night and into the next day is a firmament of sirens, questions, a car ride to the Town of Gibraltar cop shop, more questions. Turns out her name is Samantha, and she's from Green Bay. I guess they met on the Internet, probably well before I left for school.

No wonder he broke up with me.

I try to explain what I saw, but I'm accused of being drunk or high. Ma and Pa cling to each other, Ma in tears.

But not me. In fact, never me. Maybe a good cry, a cleansing cry is what I needed before writing all this down, before the shadows started dancing tonight.

I couldn't bring myself to go to the funeral, and I guess people asked about me, but not Chase's dad.

Chase's dad never speaks to my family again.

I'm home a week or so after the deaths, missing the opening lectures of my full load of classes at UW. Ma and Pa cajole me, trying to make small talk and shoehorn their way back into my life. To no avail. Finally, the minivan is idling in the driveway, and I'm heading back down the 42 to Sturgeon Bay and points beyond. We arrive on campus, and my

Goth roommate, who doesn't strike me as the touchy-feely type, greets me with a huge hug. Somehow, she already knows what happened.

The rest of the semester doesn't matter. In fact, neither do those first two years, most of which are a whirl and cadence of inebriation and seeking that higher high. Shit grades and I'm generally tuned out. I finally get the sit-down from Pa, who says, "I understand you loved Chase, but he's gone, and you'd better get your act together, because scholarships or not, personal pain or not, we can't afford UW if you're going to keep getting such poor marks."

I laugh a little at his old-fashioned parlance, but Pa remains firm.

I graduate, just barely. But professional life? Wow, I'm out of my league. I try, sure, but I start bouncing from job to job in Green Bay and end up checking groceries and living in this puny apartment out back and up the stairs from the store deep in the heart of Samantha's city. I think the owner feels sorry for me. No way rent is this cheap. Maybe he thinks he's going to get some.

I can still afford Pall Malls, though. And every night, Chase and this girl I never knew dance for me, spinning and twirling and pirouetting, locked in each others' arms like they were that night in the sky sixteen years ago, before the great and terrible fall. Like a lot of things in life, the distance of time in this case is just a few deep inhales and exhales.

The only time they stop is when I turn the kitchen light off. But I lie in my bed and can still see them dancing in my mind, somewhere high above me.

MAIDEN VOYAGE

Vestal, Ohio

The heat. The damn, ever-loving summer heat. It covered like a veil, even at 11:04 p.m., according to the clock on the squad's dash. A single drop of sweat ran from Officer Todd Fowler's hairline behind his right ear onto the collar of his navy uniform shirt, which was bear-hugged by a twenty-pound tactical vest that did nothing but absorb all that heat.

Hell of a night for my maiden voyage, he thought, as his eyes flitted from the clock to the blue-screened laptop in front of the passenger seat to the unopened bottle of Remy Martin. *Who even drinks cognac these days?* he wondered as he turned onto County Trunk Highway J. That would take him into town, to the station and the temporary holding facility, where he would Mirandize his suspect.

That suspect called himself James. *No last name, or was James his last name?* Officer Fowler couldn't get a straight answer out of the wiry, mulleted man with the thin moustache and goatee who quietly sat in the rear of the squad. The shadows created by the passing street lamps traipsed across his rugged, even handsome face, but the man said nothing. He was handcuffed, but at least he was calm. People get funny, which is to say peculiar, when it gets hot out.

Why this James guy decided to walk into Steck's Liquors at the edge of town, grab the $100 bottle of cognac, and simply walk out was beyond Officer Fowler. *Stupid criminal tricks.* When the cashier gave chase, perhaps foolishly, James clobbered him with a right uppercut that broke the man's nose and left a shirt full of blood. Then he just kept walking down the road into the heart of small-town darkness and didn't resist when Officer Fowler arrested him ten minutes later. In fact, he had even been polite: "Yes, Officer. No, Officer."

That had been a relief. Officer Fowler had completed his department's field training program the week before and was in a squad by himself for the first time. No more shadowing. It was all him, baby. He knew the book and went by it without question. In this case: Absolutely do not engage the suspect under any circumstances, and make sure the squad's mobile audio/video system is operational. If the suspect makes an utterance before the reading of his Miranda rights, remember what was said and pass it on to the detective, though the system should pick that up.

Still staring out the window, James said with nonchalance, "You know, Officer, I took a man's life tonight. I thought you should know that in case you want to investigate."

Whoa. What the hell…?

Okay, pay attention now, boy, Fowler thought, as the squad trundled down the better-lit County J. The station was about five miles away. Plenty of time for this joker to chat me up.

"I made his heart stop," James went on, making eye contact with Officer Fowler through the rearview mirror. "I think the doctors call it 'sudden cardiac arrest.' Do you know how that works?"

No response; by the book, of course. Officer Fowler goosed the accelerator just a bit. *Best get this nutcase to holding ASAP.*

"Blood is loaded with oxygen, you see, and when the heart stops beating, it can't get to the brain and other organs," James said. Was that the beginning of a smile on his face? Fowler couldn't tell in the lulls of darkness between street lamps. Sure looked like it, though.

"Death, then, happens in minutes."

Okay, this guy may be 10-96, he thought. That's cop code for a mental subject, someone who may not have the mental capacity to realize what he's said or done. Departments across the country were phasing out 10 codes in place of plain English after the chaos of Hurricane Katrina, but his chief still saw value in them for his rural Ohio department that was set in its ways. That department, by the way, hadn't had a murder in more than forty years.

Officer Fowler considered notifying Dispatch, but thought better of it, because that might indicate James was getting under his skin. Which, truth be told, he was, but like a middle-school teacher, you can't show weakness.

"I wonder, Officer, if you've ever dealt with a dead body before," James said, then squinted a bit.

"No, you're pretty young. First night on patrol by yourself, is it?"

Reflexively, Fowler turned his head, mistakenly taking his eyes off the road, because when he turned back, there he was, stumbling across County J. A tall, dark-haired, barefoot man in a torn T-shirt and blue jeans, maybe in his early forties.

Familiar. He had seen the man's face before. But where…?

"You're going to stop to help him, aren't you, Officer?" he heard James ask from the back seat behind the squad's plexiglass barrier. "Aren't you legally, and perhaps morally, obligated to do so?"

No response. *C'mon, boy*. No response.

"Officer? Officer?"

What's procedure in this situation?

The priority is the suspect in the squad. Don't leave the squad. Call Dispatch and them know what's going on. Follow and maintain visual of the subject outside the vehicle. Wait for backup. If necessary, use the loudspeaker to determine the situation.

But the man stopped in the middle of the road and held his hands high over his head. He was sweaty—who wasn't at this point of the summer?— and he had what appeared to be streaks of bloody cuts across his face and neck. One seemed to stretch like a river from his left ear to his Adam's apple.

That's who he is: Father Daniel from the First Episcopal Church downtown. Officer Fowler had met him a few weeks earlier at the church's summer carnival. They had joked about the pastor's children, ages nine, five, and three. His wife, a shapely brunette with nice legs, was really good-looking, surprising for a man of the cloth.

They lived out here somewhere, maybe across one of those farm fields. Officer Fowler remembered Father Daniel mentioning that. A parsonage. That's what it was.

"Help, Officer, help!" Father Daniel's scream carried across the sultry air as the squad came to a complete stop in front of him. He placed both hands on the hood, and the whiteness of his knuckles was apparent to Officer Fowler even in the shadows.

Father Daniel had obviously been through a lot tonight.

"Shouldn't you get out and help him?" James asked. "I mean, he's clearly in distress. Do your job. Help the man."

Instead, Fowler flipped on the loudspeaker. "Father Daniel," he said as the volume of his voice echoed voice filled the squad's cabin, "are you hurt?"

The pastor squinted at the windshield, made a fist with his right hand, and brought it to his lips while pointing with the other. "Devil!" he screamed. "Antichrist!"

It took a moment for Officer Fowler to realize the priest wasn't pointing at him; he was pointing at

James, who said, "I do believe the good Father isn't playing with a full deck, Officer. Lucifer? Please. He's a friend, but I'm not him."

"Shut up!" the officer growled, turning his head to the right, but making no eye contact with the suspect. Breach of protocol, and the system was recording away.

Damn. Do not engage the suspect. The suspect in the squad was the priority.

But was he? There were instances, according to his academy instructors, when it was appropriate to leave the squad. Maybe this was one of them…

"Devil! Antichrist! Deviiiiillll…!"

"Will you tell him I'm not Lucifer? I mean, my God," James started, but this time Officer Fowler turned almost completely around and gave him a look he hoped would have scared the crap out of a gorilla. James simply chuckled and pursed his lips into a tight, malevolent smile.

Father Daniel had taken a few steps away from the front of the squad, while Officer Fowler picked up the squad's radio microphone and fairly shouted, "Dispatch? This is 311, requesting backup at County J, a mile north of Valley Road. I'm transporting a suspect, and I have an injured subject heading north on J. I'm maintaining visual."

Nothing. Not even the crackle of static.

He tried again: nothing.

"It seems as if your colleagues have abandoned you," James said, and Fowler could still see the last vestiges of his corrupt grin before it disappeared.

"Help him, Officer Fowler," James went on. "Help him. You can save his life if you hurry. *Help him.*"

Did the suspect just use my actual name? Fowler immediately thought of his girlfriend, Ashley, and their seven-month-old son back at their crummy apartment blocks away from the First Episcopalian Church. He and Ashley were planning to get married in the fall, civil ceremony. Both of them were atheists.

"Look!" James crowed from behind.

Father Daniel had disappeared. Nothing but darkness across the windshield and hood of the squad.

Priority is the suspect: James. Protocol.

But then his thoughts turned to Father Daniel, his hot wife, and their kids.

Ashley. Their own kid who was probably snuggled in his crib at that moment.

In the dark. In the heat.

Officer Fowler gripped the door handle, stopped, looked at James in the rearview—who was still smiling—opened the door, and leapt out. *Protocol be damned.*

Father Daniel was sprawled on the pavement beside the broken yellow line that faded into the darkness beyond the range of the squad's headlights.

"Father!" he squawked, racing around the broken man's body so he faced the squad. Just in case.

Immediately, he began a heart massage. That, too, was procedure.

Father Daniel wheezed and moved his lips ever so slightly. Officer Fowler leaned in until his ear was parallel with his mouth. "B-b-banish." The priest moved no more, and his eyes became glassy slits.

"Sudden cardiac arrest," came a nearby voice now clearly outside the squad.

James was leaning on his left leg, his left hand on his hip, and the other holding the bottle of Remy Martin.

"You won't be needing this," he said as Fowler's gun unholstered itself and flew into the cornstalks on the other side of the road. James lifted his left hand, and there was what appeared to be an orange—no white—coal in the palm. He cocked his arm back as if ready to hurl it.

Officer Fowler fell backward onto his ass and pushed himself away from the suspect, who had now skip-stepped forward, apparently to gain momentum.

Now was the time. *Banish him.*

"I command you to leave!" Fowler screamed, recalling something he had read about religious wackos and their so-called ability to cast out evil spirits. *Wait, that's not enough; they always say something about Jesus.*

Therefore, the name leapt from his throat. And again and again.

"Jesus? You mean my enemy," James said, "Come on, you don't really believe in him, do you? I've been watching you for years, Officer Fowler. You don't believe in anything. Neither does Ashley. And neither will your boy. That will be your legacy after you join me in my dwelling.

"Now, Father Daniel is a true believer, which is why I came to call on him tonight. True believers are tough nuts to crack, but if you apply enough pressure… It was amazingly simple to lure him into the cornstalks from his 'parsonage.' I merely whispered in his ear and told him to come."

A pause.

"And yes, I lied. I am the god of this world. I am he of which the good Father spoke." James raised his left arm again, and this time the spherical coal in his hand made for Officer Fowler's chest.

Maybe my vest will ward it off, he thought. *Doubtful.* There was no time.

"Jesus!" he screamed once again.

At that, the hot coal burst into a million tiny pieces illuminated by the glare of the squad's headlights. They bounced on the pavement between

Fowler and Father Daniel, like cigarette ash, before flaming out.

Suddenly James was gone along with the bottle of Remy Martin.

The suspect. The suspect was supposed to be the priority.

A siren began to wail in the distance, getting closer. Backup.

Maybe the radio had actually worked.

But Dispatch didn't acknowledge me. How is that possible? How is any of this possible?

There was a cough, a wheeze, really, and Officer Fowler darted toward Father Daniel, who wasn't moving, but he was alive.

"Officer," came a weak, thready voice, "help me."

Fowler crawled on his hands and knees across the pavement to where the Father lie; the bloody marks were still evident on his face and neck. They looked worse up close: clear, precision cuts that might have been made by a doctor with a scalpel or even a mortician or medical examiner.

He wasn't going to make it. That was clear.

"Officer…"

"Yes, Father."

"Let the Lord guide you."

***

The department's inquiry of the event, which received assistance from both county and state law enforcement, took a month. Officer Fowler didn't need the book to tell him that honesty was the best policy in this situation. His mother had taught him that. He truthfully responded to every question, every cross-examination, every angry missive by men who were trained to root out untruth. But they could find none. For that, Officer Fowler received a thirty-day suspension without pay, but at least he retained his job.

In the intervening time, he attended Father Daniel's funeral, hugged his widow and their three children, and cried like everyone else. He and Ashley made it through the toughest financial month of their lives with a little help from both sets of parents, and they started planning their marriage ceremony, which would be held the following spring at First Episcopal Church. And a surprise: they were expecting again. Her doctor said it was another boy, whom they decided to name Daniel.

Officer Fowler was relegated to a desk after he returned to work, and that bright autumn day, the receptionist informed him that Father Daniel's wife was in the lobby. He went up front, and as usual, she was stunning in a pair of white capri pants and a sleeveless blouse. Her youngest was in tow and clearly bored. In her hand was a rectangular package with Officer Fowler's name on it in black magic marker.

She explained that it had been left on her front porch, and since it was addressed to him, she figured she should drop it off, yada yada.

Fowler opened the box, and inside was a bottle of Remy Martin and a note that read, "I told you I took a man's life that night."

CEO

Menlo Park, California

Artemis Hoover leaned forward in his chair at the head of the burnished conference room table, folded his arms, and said, "I'm not shy. I'll address the elephant in the room." His eyes bored like two red lasers into Tap, Inc.'s CEO Amy Jameson, who sat at the opposite end of the table next to a television monitor with the social media network's red T app logo.

She hadn't even had the opportunity to begin her quarterly earnings update.

"Amy, are you an alien?" came the simple question from Hoover, a heavyset man in his early seventies, today wearing an impeccable charcoal Brooks Brothers suit with a red power tie. A class ring with the same color stone was on the third finger of his right hand, like another evil eye.

Amy had anticipated the question; she still had allies on the board. But she feigned surprise. "I fail to see how that question has any relevance to today's meeting or any meeting, for that matter," she replied, returning his lasers with an icy counterpunch.

"I think it has everything to do with this meeting and your presentation," Hoover went on, clearly struggling to remain collegial. "There are rumors on the street that you're M'Lon. I don't think I have to remind you of the embarrassment that such a revelation would do to our stock price, especially for the biggest social media company on this planet. Our brand would immediately fall under the category of subversive."

M'Lon. The word hung like stench in the closed conference room, even eliciting a quiet "Oooh" from the middle of the table.

The M'Lon galactic voyagers had arrived at Earth some ten years ago in mile-long V-shaped ships. As a species, they were exactly like humans, down to the DNA level. But their ungainly conduct, lack of clothing, and severely broken English had immediately made them second-class citizens of a cosmopolitan Earth. Their reputation was quickly exacerbated by the explosion of conversation on Tap and the planet's few other insignificant social networks, along with cracks on late-night TV. The bastardized word "mollen" had become a racist pejorative.

However, the M'Lon were barred from holding any political or corporate position on Earth for one simple fact: They were ardent, near-fanatical worshippers of their god, a tangible machine the size of a quarter of their home planet, which is approximately two light years from the star Proxima Centauri.

There was a danger in allowing aliens, who may be taking orders from a self-aware machine, to hold positions of power on Earth. Besides, the concept of deity worship had become passé on Earth. Outmoded thinking.

"You know there are no reliable blood tests to determine whether one is human or M'Lon, Art," Amy said. "So you'll have to take my word." Now it was Amy who sat forward in her chair. "I do not have M'Lon blood coursing through my veins," she said "And with all due respect to you and this board, I resent the implication."

That was true. Amy Jameson was indeed human. But Artemis Hoover hated liars. He had built his personal brand on his honesty, and as such, had worked to root out falsehood in the organizations he had led. Retired now, that transcended to his board leadership.

"Come on, Amy, you know companies all over Silicon Valley have alien trash working at the highest levels," he said. "When it comes out, those companies suffer. Stock prices drop, layoffs ensue, and some even die a slow death."

Now he stood, and his gut sagged over the waistband of his pants. "You see, Amy, it's all about perception," he said. "You might be an alien or you might not. I, for one, have my doubts, but regardless, if Tap's CEO isn't perceived as a machine worshipper yet, it's coming; mark my words. That's why I'm compelled to ask this board for a vote, right now, on terminating Amy Jameson as CEO."

Amy had anticipated the tenor of this meeting, and as a Dartmouth-educated strategist, she had studied it from every conceivable angle. Thus, she was prepared for her response to a vote.

She paused, a PR trick to command attention. "Do what you must," she finally said. "I let the results speak for me." She pressed a button on a console, and the monitor behind her showed a bar graph with the quarterly growth in stock price over the past two years of her tenure. The range was considerable. A 4.2-percent increase in first quarter led all the way to a 12.3-percent jump in the most recent quarter.

The next slide showed another bar graph with similar increases in new users, especially internationally, and for the first time, intergalactically. The final slide was a pie chart that depicted wild growth in advertising revenue.

Artemis Hoover was voted down. It wasn't even close.

Hours later, Amy Jameson poured a glass of Merlot as her twins raced around the kitchen island. Her life partner, a tall, goateed man with warm eyes named Jeff, leaned against the island with his arms folded.

"So you're still employed," he said. "That's a relief."

One of the twins did a hard turn around the corner and crashed into an open drawer and started to cry.

"Nouakchott! Ah fenza foopala…!"

"Stop!" Amy implored. "We don't speak M'Lon around here. Do you want the kiddos to go to school and have everyone think they're alien?"

"Sorry, sorry," Jeff said, patting the twin on the booty and encouraging him to go back to play.

"So what else happened today?" she said, pouring another glass.

"I got a transmission from home," he replied. "God wants you to introduce a new feature on Tap that will turn conversational sentiment toward at least the possibility of a M'Lon presidency. Think you can do that?"

"I can do anything I want," she said. "I'm the CEO, after all."

"If you haven't had a bitter period and survived it, you can't feel true satisfaction. You end up accepting the world around you rather than relishing it."

—Hu Guohui

GRIEFER

South Philadelphia, Pennsylvania

An avatar of some white wannabe ghetto gangster wearing a straight-billed Devils cap: hey you jersey fuck do the world a favor & off yourself

Post.

A long echo-chamber thread extolling the virtues of the iPhone X: fuck tha iphone lets talk bout tha Samsung S9 its tha bomb

Post.

A butch middle-aged woman wearing what looked like a faded Melissa Etheridge concert T from way back when: lezbo

Post.

Then a retaliatory response by her so off-color, decorum dictates it shouldn't be repeated here.

(With the inflection of a Nubian queen in his head): Oh no, you di'in't!

Tappity tap tap.

SKANKY LEZZY WHORE!!!!!!!!!

Aanndd…post. Then block.

There. That's better. First find the bastards, then pile on. Obliterate anybody who resists. The strategy: Hit and run. Stick and move.

For Josh trolling was like being the sheriff of an unruly Old West town. There were undesirables walking *his* streets, and they needed to be on that virtual stagecoach headed out of town. Get that shit out the door. Because people, man… On Twitter, people expose their weaknesses as if they were virtues. Same with Facebook, Instagram, YouTube, Snap, all of them. People were avatar faces just begging for a double-barreled response to posts that were all kinds of stupid. They were soiling the dusty streets of *his* world.

Bitches. Foreigners. Wimps. Blimps. Snowflakes. The obvious assholes. And especially the Bible thumpers.

They were all alike. They *needed* policing, and he was Wyatt Earp. As a matter of fact, that was his handle: @earp666DDT. The 666 part, a holdover from his days as an evangelical, added that little bit of sinister, a bumper tap of the apocalyptic. DDT? That was just for fun. That stuff will mess you up.

Josh's avatar was his calling card—a pic of him wearing a cowboy hat atop an S&M mask, the kind with square eyeholes and a zipper for the mouth. He bought it at a dark place simply called Leather tucked away off Broad Street when he was a junior at 'Nova, after he took a short course called Social Media Branding.

He co-opted the principles to his own situation: Select the right channels (all of them, even

LinkedIn); develop your own voice (assertive, decisive); use visuals (GIFs from *Dumb and Dumber* and *Family Guy* were his favorites, along with porn, naturally); and most of all, post regularly. First thing in the morning to get everyone off to a paranoid start, because who wants to know they're going to be stalked all day by Wyatt Earp, and those desperate hours at 3:00 a.m. when the suicidals were just begging to be pushed over the edge.

He was a brand. And with thousands of followers on all of his platforms, just waiting to see what bizarro shit he was going to pull next, it was a rush. Better than any pot or coke he had ever indulged in. Deep down, while he had gotten off on the reckless abandon of drugs as a kid, he quickly became cognizant of the possibility of addiction, which is why he made the decision to shift online and become a keyboard cowboy in a cyber-western.

But the best part? Anonymity. *That* was the real high.

What was behind the curtain wasn't all that glamorous. He haunted a cubicle from nine to five, cold calling potentials, 95% of which hung up on him. The particularly challenging ones, the ones who were curt or got wise, ended up with an online visit from @earp666DDT, guns blazing. They didn't know what hit them, ever. And of course, he got blocked aplenty, but that was the price you paid for being a social media antihero. Check that: a social media archvillain.

"Josh, the reports, please," a stern, balding man said as he arrived soundlessly at his cube, the taupe carpet masking black wingtips. Baldy was Marty Sharafinski, Sr., the Polack who owned Gold

Industries, Philadelphia's leading provider of cleaning supplies to the city and the tristate area's corporate wonks. Josh was one of his faceless sales lackeys, a millennial stuck behind a gaggle of Gen-Xers, lifers satisfied with their ranches and bungalows in Rittenhouse and Pointe Breeze. That included Marty's son, Marty Jr., who lived in an elegant Cape Cod in Chesterbrook and was being groomed for the top spot, all but ensuring things probably wouldn't change.

"Working on them, boss man," Josh blithely replied, hitting the minimize button on his web browser, his Twitter feed tornadoing off the screen. Baldy was a baby boomer late in his tenure as president and CEO, but he still took his job as seriously as he did on day one and pushed his sales guys to mine deeper into an already crowded marketplace, including (and perhaps especially) Josh. Sure, there was a rush in hooking a fatty like the Art Institute of Philadelphia, which Josh had secured six months ago, but while he was still riding that high, Marty Sharafinski, Sr. clearly wasn't. Sales team huddles were a scowl fest in his direction.

Plus, that bow-tied prune didn't have one social media account, ranting and railing that social was a total waste of time.

But if he had…

"Could you kindly have them on my desk by three?" Baldy said with the inflection of a demand more than a request. To emphasize his point, he stared at Josh just a moment longer, like the parent of a recalcitrant child might when he's trying to emphasize a subtle point.

"Yeah, you got it," Josh replied, tapping his keyboard. *Come on, come on. Get out of my world*, he thought, and the boss finally soundlessly stalked off toward Marty Jr.'s corner office.

Josh had to get out of there. Plain and simple. But that was a problem for another day.

At present, there was a mark to deal with.

The elderly guy with a black brim atop a crown of silver hair and leathery hands gripping a wooden cane had stood out to Josh for the fact that he was, what, in his eighties, and on Twitter? *Please.* Most people getting up in age spent their virtual time on Facebook, keeping in touch with their children (not grandkids, who were on Snap and Instagram) and their dying high school classmates. But this person was a frequent poster, several times a day, sharing pics of his shih tzu, apparently named Skippy, along with extravagant meals he ate at swank joints like the Hungry Pigeon and Vernick's.

Josh surmised his wife had died recently because there were several pathetic posts from a few months earlier showing him and a woman about his age doing things that retirees do: bumbling down a winding street in Paris, hosting Easter, flanking Bobby Vinton at a nightclub in Vegas, sharing a Tastykake Snowball with shit-eating grins on their faces. But the dead giveaway was a simple post of a poorly digitized photo. He was wearing a tux and tails and she a veil. The words, See you soon, my Polish princess, sandwiched the photo and his handle, @mikolaj.

Polish princess? Really?

Oh yeah. This was going to be fun. Guy would never know what hit him. Wouldn't know what to do. Probably wouldn't even know how to block him.

The first post: was she good in bed

Next: i'd a banged her back then

Finally: prolly in hell by now

That last one harked back to his dubious evangelical roots. Josh grew up in a born-again, tongue-talkin', as-for-me-and-my-house-we'll-serve-the-Lord existence. He had shitcanned all that garbage years ago and was an atheist now, but old people still filled churches and were afraid of fairy tales. There was no heaven or hell; he had dismissed that claptrap as a teenager, but it was fun yanking chains, especially the decrepit souls living on borrowed time who had no damn business wandering *his* streets at night.

Every moment was night.

It took almost an hour to get a response, but it wasn't a surprise: Leave me alone, you punk!

A punk? *That's the best you can do? Let's try this*: i bet you jack of to her pic

(If you're wondering, punctuation was never Josh's strong suit.)

Then he added: can you even get it up these dayz?

The response: You're going to be sorry.

Josh: i'm sure

And then, a surprise: Romans 12:19

Josh frowned. Sounded vaguely familiar, like it was on the tip of his tongue but he just couldn't elucidate. He logged onto Bible.com, which defaulted to the King James Version: "Dearly beloved, avenge not yourselves, but rather give place unto wrath: for it is written, Vengeance is mine; I will repay, saith the Lord."

Is that a threat?

The Nubian queen again: Oh no, he di'in't!

And then, the *coup de grâce* from the old man: a smiley face emoji! ʊ

An emoji? Insolence! This guy is begging for a showdown at high noon in the middle of Twitter's dusty Main Street, the rest of the avatars cowering behind virtual clapboard buildings, horses, and water troughs.

Of course, Josh responded in kind, and once again, decorum doesn't allow what he posted here. But there was no response. None. Guy didn't even block him. Twenty-three posts later, Josh got bored and moved on to some slag with sandy-brown hair who had made the mistake of posting a few bikini pics on her feed. He shamed her for awhile until she blocked him, then he decided to hit Subway for lunch. About all he could afford.

That was the thing. Josh had invested in the right car (a used silver Beemer, license plate WYATT

E) and the right place (a condo in trendy South Philly), expecting the payoff within a year of starting at Gold, but he was coming up on a year and there was no end in sight to the bills piling up on his dining room table and maxed-out credit cards. Obviously, Marty Sr. had everything to do with that, not to mention the corporate culture he had fashioned in which his young Gen-X turks got all the best accounts and left him with the scraps, although the art institute *had* been a coup and should have been the gateway to a larger world.

Didn't happen.

He ordered a foot-long, double-meat, grilled Spicy Italian on flatbread and scrolled Twitter.

The old man, @mikolaj, had actually followed him.

No eff'ing way.

Josh blocked him and sat down to dive into his sandwich. Through the first greasy mouthful he checked Facebook. Let's see… a bunch of malignant responses to posts he had made when he arrived at work and a friend request.

The old man. A one Mr. Mikolaj. No first name. Or was it last name?

Come on! Seriously? The old man has stones.

Josh found his feed and posted: like I said, ur wife wuz a whore

The response: Romans 12:19

And one more thing: ʊ

Josh just shook his head, went to settings and blocked him, then toggled back to Twitter. He had a bunch of responses to recent posts, mostly vile, along with eleven new followers. Right there, the fifth one down, was the old man, but this time with the handle @mikolaj68.

Four below that was the same avatar with the handle @mikolaj14.

Blocked and blocked. This was obviously not the old man, who couldn't possible that savvy, but perhaps somebody Josh had pissed off, and as for who that might be, the line starts to the left. But it could also be one of his own boys, maybe one of his 'Nova roommates, who like him, had a penchant for online thuggery. Swipe an avatar from somewhere on the net, throw up a bunch of accounts on Twitter and Facebook, and have fun fucking with people.

It's what Josh did every day.

Thus, there was a sudden familiarity that made Josh smile as he gulped the last part of his sandwich and dabbed his lips to remove the excess mayo, then cursed as he realized he had dribbled something on his cherry power tie. As he scrolled, he got another follower, @mikolaj745—and then another, @mikolaj221. It would all be good banter over beers and bowls with his boys whenever they got together. In fact, maybe one of his boys was making a point: Where'd you go? It's been awhile. We've got to get together.

Mental note: call the boys and set something up

over the weekend at the condo.

Back to Facebook. Another friend request, this time from another Mikolaj account with the same avatar. Click on settings, block, move on.

Instagram. Same thing, @mikolaj. This was getting hysterical.

The time caught Josh's eye: 12:52 p.m. *Damn.* Team huddle in eight minutes, and if he was late, there would be another Marty Sr. scowl fest.

Two-and-a-half minutes later he was huffing and puffing on the elevator chugging along floor by floor, dinging as each one went by. *Come on, come on. Sixth floor. Hurry up.* Baldy's gonna be pissed.

Of course someone got on at the fifth floor. Oh God. It was that HR skag who had processed him in a year ago. She had breath that smelled like underarm and flowery blouses with a whiff of mothballs. Based on principle alone, Josh had invaded her Facebook account and set things right, before someone taught her how to block him. In the 'vator, they exchanged pleasantries, she asking how things were going, and he noting that he saw her on Facebook and just loved the pic of her flowers.

"Oh, that's my garden," she said. "My pride and joy."

Sure it is.

Josh arrived just as Baldy was starting the huddle, and of course, he got the scowl. Gonna be a long next hour discussing the dangerous world of sales strategy and, of course, numbers, numbers, numbers. "Always be closing," Baldy was fond of saying, which was from some stupid movie from the '80s Josh had never seen. What Josh didn't get was how Baldy could demand his monthly sales recap by 3:00 p.m., yet drone on until well after 2:00 p.m., giving him barely enough time to get it done. There was always a Steve Jobs end to each meeting: "…oh, and one more thing…," usually an inspirational quote or some other exhortation to do better, do more, do right. Deliver.

The mind in a meeting is often like a runner, wending its way from one off-topic thing to another: gotta pick up my dry cleaning; what should we have for dinner tonight? I'm gonna break up with her this weekend. Josh's went something like this:

Need to a new strategy for Instagram;

Lost twenty-some followers there this week;

Do I need a new avatar?

Facebook is sooo lame;

Got an idea for a new YouTube series;

Who's the old man?

His Galaxy dinged loudly as Marty Sr. dove into a reminder speech about the difference between sales *strategy* and sales *tactics* and how both tied back to marketing. Everyone looked at Josh for a moment and then brought their eyes collectively back to the boss, who tried to ignore the interruption, but wrinkled his nose in a way a child might after smelling Brussels sprouts for the first time.

Josh grabbed the phone and fumbled to toggle it to buzz; that was on him for not doing so before the meeting, but oh well. As he was doing that, it dinged again and again.

Baldy stopped and stared.

"Something wrong, Josh?" Curt.

"Nope, just messages from potential customers," he said, pivoting into charm mode, which occasionally worked with Marty Sr. and almost always with the cavalcade of millennial women who graced his bed at the condo. Apparently it worked this time because the man didn't miss a beat, picking up his stream of consciousness like a train might reenter the tracks from a branch line.

The phone went to near-constant buzz over the next forty-five minutes, so much so that Josh eventually had to slip it into his back pocket because it kept bouncing on the table. It wasn't surprising, really. Such was life in a troll's world, especially for the self-styled cyber Wyatt Earp. Sure as hell wasn't customers calling, but what did Baldy know? There was relative safety in the sense that if Baldy thought Josh was putting forth his best effort, then certain things could be overlooked, at least for now. Perception was reality in this case. Josh just wasn't sure how long that would last. Put a gun to his head—a six-shooter, maybe?—and he might reveal that deep down he felt he was on borrowed time at Gold Industries. Which is why he had to get out first.

The huddle finally ended with another Jobsian

cliffhanger, this time a quote from the man himself. "Great things in business are never done by one person," Marty Sr. said. "Your work is going to fill a large part of your life, and the only way to be truly satisfied is to do what you believe is great work." Like everyone else in the room, Josh nodded fervently, looking around the table at guys he didn't like and couldn't respect.

As his counterparts began filing out, Josh pulled out his phone and checked the prompts.

There were hundreds of them. He started scrolling and the same words filled the screen until they seemed to unite as one, like a film reel: Mikolaj is now following you.

The Galaxy S9 bounced on the dark-stained oak table, leaving a mark big enough to reflect the overhead light.

No wonder there was so much buzzing.

What the fu…? His inner monologue trailed off. Who's got time to individually create hundreds of Twitter accounts with slightly different handles and then start following a dude like Josh?

He unlocked the phone, clicked the Twitter icon, and sure as shit, the follows were legit. But here's a flash: the individual accounts he clicked on, probably two dozen of them before he dropped the phone again, had thousands of tweets like just about every other normal Twitter account. In other words, this wasn't some bullshit being perpetrated by his boys for laughs. This was an elaborate, probably coordinated attack. Maybe from offshore. Russians?

Chinese?

Let's not get dramatic.

Okay, Josh thought, *it's cool.* There's a way out of this. Has to be. But the only viable option seemed to be individually blocking them all, a likely never-ending task, considering the fact that six more follows from accounts with the same avatar and slightly different handles arrived while he was scrolling. Every minute or so, one more. Sure, he could go to Twitter's Help Center and lodge an abuse complaint, but they never responded, and their model was designed to deal with one account at a time. Not hundreds of them. Probably would take one look at his account and laugh at a griefer's lament.

He slouched in his chair and frowned.

Eyebrows slowly raised, eyes bugged.

What about Facebook? What about all of the other platforms?

Hand shaking, he clicked the Facebook icon and the app flashed open.

Four hundred and fifty-three friend requests.

From?

To be fair, a few were legit, you might say one out of every thirty or forty. But the same face stared back at him, a wrinkled countenance with a toothy grin and a beret cocked slightly to the right. The same name.

Holy shit, holy shit, holy shit. This can't be happening.

Josh randomly chose one of the accounts and clicked. The most recent post was from that morning at 10:13 a.m. from Love Park; the monolithic sculpture's red letters appeared just behind his right earlobe, and the fountain graced the left. Someone had taken that photo, so someone out there knew who this guy was. He scrolled down and the same banal crap that people post was there, including the chestnut-hued photo of the Polish princess posted two weeks earlier.

He selected another account and clicked. This time, the most recent post was also made at 10:13 a.m., but he was in front of the Liberty Bell this time.

Another. 10:13 a.m. Independence Hall.

Yet another. 10:13 a.m. Leaning against a column of the Art Institute of Philadelphia, and for a passing moment, Josh painfully reminisced about all the times he had gone down there to seal his sales deal, the hours spent in sweaty negotiations before finally, finally, getting the approval. Damn, that was a lot of work for one sale.

The phone dinged. Snap coming in.

"I told you you'd be sorry, punk," the old man said, then chuckled as a grandfather would if a child had said something inappropriate. "I know who's behind that leather mask of yours. Right, Josh?"

Okay, this was new.

How does this guy know my actual name? And if he knows that…

Heart sinking. Beads of sweat. Shaking hands. The whole deal.

The earmarks of realization.

Josh looked down at his phone. The Snap had disappeared, which shouldn't have happened that fast.

"Josh, I'm expecting those reports by three," Marty Sr.'s raised voice carried from the hallway outside the conference room, cutting through the cyber din like a knife through warm butter.

Josh turned toward the doorway, but Baldy had strode on, leaving words in his wake that sounded something like, "…better get with it, son…"

Maybe that was it? Work. *Gotta get to work. Gotta take my mind off this.*

Whatever's happening will work itself out.

Plus, he did have those reports to do, and he'd have to put the pedal to the metal to get them done in forty minutes. So in the interest of his condo, the Beemer, and a false sense of maturity, he did the one thing that he swore he would never be cowed into doing by anybody.

He turned his phone off.

That was the loser's way out of dealing with trolls like him. Just kill the phone for awhile and hope they get bored and go away.

Boy, it hurt.

But he was on the ropes, and it was astounding that some old dick was the perp.

Five minutes later, after hitting the crapper, he was back at his desk, feverishly diving into spreadsheets and migrating the data to a Word doc he'd email to Baldy by 3:00 p.m. Or maybe just slightly thereafter, because come on, give a guy a break, a grace period. It wasn't fair to ask someone to go to meetings all day and then get some stupid report done by some randomly chosen time.

Baldy had to learn he wasn't a puppet master. He might be the owner, the boss, the grand pooh-bah, whatever, but yanking marionette strings just for his own entertainment? Wasn't going to happen. No way.

The email arrived at 2:47 p.m. as Josh was toggling from one spreadsheet to another, copying and pasting, and trying to focus his energies into writing analyses that made sense, at least to him.

It was from mikolaj@gmail.com. The subject line was: Romans 12:19.

Uh-uh. No, no, no.

He slumped back into his captain's chair—one of his demands during the interview process way back when—and let his head fall backward to stare at the ceiling.

He opened the email, which said: See you soon, punk.

Below was a JPEG of the old man's avatar photo. It was bigger, of course, and Josh could tell it was taken outside Citizens Bank Park by the fencing that cordoned off the main entrance of the Phillies' home.

The signature line simply said: Mikolaj.

Josh: listen motherfucker, u better be sure u dont slip up, cuz Ill kill u

It was 2:54 p.m. His phone intercom chirped, and Baldy's nasal voice drifted into his cubicle, "Where are those reports, Josh?" Clearly annoyed.

Ef 'im. I still have six minutes. Josh pressed Send.

"On the way, boss," he said, then clicked on one of his three spreadsheets before he noticed a silent response in his inbox: Undeliverable.

WTF?

The intercom. "Josh, come to my office, please."

"Can you give me a minute, boss, I'm just fini…"

"Now, Josh." The thud of Baldy's handset hanging up.

Another email from mikolaj@gmail.com as he was standing up: I told you you'd be sorry. And under it: ℧

The intercom again: "Josh."

"Coming."

He sauntered into Baldy's office, and the man said nothing, but motioned him to a wooden armchair in front of his beautifully stained oak desk, probably a holdover from the company founder. That skag HR lady was in the chair next to his, looking pensive and clutching a bunch of file folders to her chest. From behind him, he heard the door close gently, which brought up Josh's heart rate and made his palms sweat.

Not happening, not happening not…

"Josh, we're letting you go. The position isn't meeting our expectations," Baldy said, sitting up in his chair and crossing his arms on his manual day planner, stained with coffee rings and marked up with inks of different colors. An absent thought: *He doesn't use his phone for appointments?*

"When you're in my position and you hire somebody, certain expectations come with it," he went on. "The main thing, not only for our company, but for any company, is sales. We need consistent sales to pay salaries and, of course, make a profit. Your ability to generate sales has been, let's say, lackluster. I need someone in your position who can make his numbers on a consistent basis. I understand there will be an off month once in awhile, but your off months are the norm rather than exception."

"But," Josh started, and was unceremoniously

cut off.

"It's purely about numbers," Baldy said. "But I have to tell you, I often get the feeling that your mind is somewhere else, like you'd rather be anywhere but here. I can't have that in your position, so…"

"This isn't fair!" Josh bleated, and even he thought he sounded like a middle-schooler who had just gotten grounded. "I busted my ass for this company! I got you the Art Institute!"

"That was good," Baldy said, "but this isn't really about me. It's about the institution that is Gold Industries. Steve Jobs once said, 'Some people aren't used to an environment where excellence is expected.'"

"Oh. My. God. You're pulling out a fu…, a Steve Jobs quote as you *fire* me?"

"Come on, Josh, it's for the best. I really think you'll be happier elsewhere."

"No, I won't. I need this, sir. Please!"

Baldy readjusted his backside in his seat, then stood up, and reached across his desk, grabbing a photo in a sleek sterling silver frame. He held it in one hand and stared at it wistfully. "My father came over here from Poland after the war and started this company," he said. "He was in a death camp, and when he got out, he only weighed eighty pounds. He should have died, but he always used to tell me that every day, every person is a gift from God. But he was also a tough businessman and had no qualms removing someone who didn't fit. And I just don't think you fit, Josh."

"Can I have another chance? I swear I will make this right. I…"

Baldy turned the photo around. It was the old man, his grin seeming to gloat now as he peered over his cane at Josh.

"He's dead now, but it's his legacy I have to be mindful of."

Josh just stared.

"Do you get it?" Baldy asked. "Do you?"

STANDBY

According to the monitor, Flight 777 was listed as "Delayed." Originally, it had been scheduled to take off at 9:00 a.m. CST, but now departure had been moved to 10:30 a.m. Sherman gripped his wooden cane and shuddered just a little.

Ninety minutes. What was a ninety-six-year-old man going to do with ninety minutes of free time in a Podunk airport? This wasn't O'Hare, with its four massive terminals, or even Midway, with one terminal but three concourses, which makes it feel bigger than it actually is.

Oh well, he thought. *At least I have a seat on the most important flight of my life.*

Destination: Heaven.

The monitor switched screens and listed what looked to be endless names: the standby list. Sherman was sure glad he wasn't on standby and pitied those who were.

What were your options if you couldn't get on the plane? It wasn't like you could go home and come back tomorrow.

Since his hip replacement, he had learned to pivot on his good leg so he could turn with relative ease as long as he had his cane, which had belonged to his father and his grandfather before that. It was dark wood with just enough scratches and marks from heavy usage over the decades to give it…personality. Sherman hoped someday his only begotten son would be able to use it, although that would mean he would be closing in on his own airport destination.

Sherman turned and nearly ran into a woman who breezed up behind him to stare at the monitor. She was middle-aged with blonde, curly hair and an air of confidence, possibly even assertiveness or maybe even arrogance, as if she belonged here.

"Oh brother," she said, crestfallen. "The flight's delayed?" The screen switched, and her jaw dropped. "Standby?" she fairly yelled. "I'm on standby? That can't be right. After all I did to advance the Kingdom, and I'm on *standby*?"

She nearly ran over to the podium in her mid-sized heels, where a pleasant woman from the airline in a blue vest and a red scarf looked her up on the computer. Sherman could see the counter worker nodding back and forth as the blonde woman waved her arms around in apparent dismay.

Standby.

This wasn't a tantrum like Sherman had seen once at O'Hare, when a young businessman couldn't get on his flight to Los Angeles. Apparently, the man had an important meeting, and after cursing out the airline representative with some of the most vile language Sherman had ever heard, he threw down his briefcase in disgust. It opened and all of his important papers spilled out on the wine-colored carpeting in front of the podium.

That was so long ago.

I wonder whatever happened to him? Sherman thought as he doddered over to the Chili's near the concourse, which already looked filled to capacity.

***

The blonde woman's name was Brenda, and she had accepted the Lord in high school. She started going to a born-again, tongue-talking Pentecostal church after the divorce and, henceforth, had devoted the rest of her natural life to advancing "the Kingdom." She was in church every Sunday morning and evening and every Wednesday evening, as well, with Bible study on Fridays. She ran the A/V booth at her church and was always the first to sign up for door-to-door witnessing. Whenever a prominent Word of Faith preacher came to town, she coordinated a fleet of school buses to get the entire church congregation there.

Can't make it? Mm-hmm. Priorities, priorities, she would think when some church brothers and sisters turned her down. At least her soul was at peace. Gotta soak up that Word.

In other words, Brenda was busy, busy, busy for the Lord, and she loved the fast pace and quick decision making that had gone along with it. There was always something to do, always some church committee to chair, always some campaign to support. Always someone to direct and, sometimes, correct.

Until early this morning, when she arrived here, at the airport. It took some time to get through security, and she lightly protested when they took away her carry-on, but the TSA agent's joke—"Here, you really *can't* take it with you, heh-heh"—had placated her. There was a bit of angst, though, when they whisked away the pink tote she received free for purchasing a pile of books and CDs at a Joyce Meyer crusade years ago, which she had embroidered with words from Luke 6:38: *Give and it will be given to you.*

Losing her tote she could handle. But standby. Come on. *Standby!* After all those hours and that tithing, this was her eternal reward?

The airline lady behind the podium, a brunette whose nametag read "Roz," was collegial and professional. Brenda had insisted it was a mix-up; couldn't Roz please check her computer to be extra sure?

After looking, Roz told her she was number 315 on the standby list, so while it was unlikely she would make the 10:30 a.m. flight, if a seat did open up, her name would be announced.

"So stay nearby," Roz said. "I recommend the Chili's over there. See it? Where that older gentleman with the cane is going? Wait there and maybe get a bite to eat. I've had the three-egg omelet with asparagus and goat cheese, and it's divine. No pun intended." Another warm smile.

Brenda sighed, turned on her heel, and walked briskly to the restaurant. She had nearly made it to the entrance when Roz's tinny voice came through over the public address system, with the official announcement that Flight 777 had been delayed. A chorus of *Awww* followed.

Chili's was packed. The bar was three deep with people ordering mimosas and Bloody Marys, even a few flutes of champagne. *Tsk-tsk*, Brenda thought. *Lost souls. How did they ever end up here, in the airport, to begin with? If I'm on standby, then they certainly are.*

Others were crowded around the dozen or so tables in the dining area, the enticing smell of breakfast food wafting over them. A group invited the old man with the cane to take a seat in a chair next to the wall under a mural of the famous Chili's red pepper. Another man, younger with a turban and a curly black beard, spied Brenda and stood, offering her his seat. She sat and said nothing, but made eye contact with the old man, who was on her left with both hands on the top of his cane.

*****

Sherman's eyesight wasn't what it once was, but the blonde woman was striking, if not exactly friendly. He greeted her, but she apparently hadn't heard him because she turned away to look toward the gate. When she turned back, he said hello again, and this time she acknowledged the pleasantry with barely a crack of a smile.

"You're on standby, ain'a?" he said, and with that, the crack went away. Clearly not pleased, but Sherman plowed forward anyway. "Don't worry about it," he said, trying to be upbeat. "Golly, if I can make it on a flight, then pretty much anybody can."

The woman furrowed her brow, as if this was some sort of revelation. "What do you mean by that?" she said, not in an aggressive tone, but heading in that direction.

"Well, I only mean that I wasn't perfect. I did a lot of things I regret now. And I mean a lot. I still managed to get a seat. You'll get on, too, my dear. Try not to worry about it."

Flustered, the woman asked a strange question: "Are you born again?"

At this, Sherman responded with a quizzical look, a cross between a smile and a frown. "Not sure what you mean by that," he said, having to raise his voice an octave due to a crowd of loud young men who had just entered. "I'm just a simple man."

The woman just shrugged and shook her head. "See, that's what I mean. Of anybody here, including you, I should be on that flight. I've *got* to get on that flight. I don't know what I'll do if I can't. Where am I supposed to go?"

That's the $64,000 question, Sherman thought. When he had arrived at the terminal, he had walked past dozens of people languishing in the black-leather seats that lined each gate. No headphones, magazines, or anything. Just sitting and staring straight ahead, utterly inert. Didn't even look like they were breathing, to tell the truth.

"There's plenty of time," he offered, looking at his watch, an old Bulova model that had been his brother's, which he had received after Richard was killed in the war. "It's only 9:10 a.m."

"Are you trying to make me feel better?" she shot back. "Because it's not working." She concluded her remark with a faux chuckle that was meant to be sarcastic. Sherman knew that at least.

"Now, now. No need to be hasty," he replied. "I'm just trying to make conversation."

"Yeah, well…don't."

She stood up, and looked again toward the gate just as a waitress came to the table, introduced herself, and asked if anyone would like something to drink.

"I don't suppose you have a beer—Pabst?" Sherman said. "Probably going to be my last one. May as well make it memorable. Say…"

The blonde woman turned around and said, "What?"

"Can I get you something to drink?"

***

The last thing Brenda needed in this situation was a drink. She had had a few wild nights in college and occasionally enjoyed a glass of wine during the early, happy days of her marriage. But once she'd accepted the Lord after the divorce, that all went away. *For the better,* she added to herself.

"No," she said to that old, unsaved fool as she sat down again, "I don't want a drink. I don't drink. You shouldn't either."

He gripped his cane, adjusted his backside in his seat, and responded with a kind smile. "Suit yourself," he said. "Just trying to pass the time before the flight."

The flight. Standby.

Her heart sank again, and she flashed another glance at the gate, but she couldn't see it because a bunch of loud college-aged boys had just bellied up the bar, laughing about some party they had recently attended and the drive home that apparently turned into a wild adventure. *Probably going to drink this place dry*, she thought.

It isn't fair. I gave everything for the Lord and the church. Everything!

Now I'm here in this…this…place, with all these heathen people who never gave the Lord a second glance in their lives.

Is this airport purgatory like the Catholics believed?

Or…no, no, no, it couldn't be! Is this hell?

That didn't make any sense, though. She had repeated the words of the salvation prayer with pastor the first day she went to church, a warm, bright May Sunday.

She had been a sinner, it was true. But she had been redeemed.

That *was* truth.

The waitress showed up with the older gentleman's beer, a Pabst Blue Ribbon, along with a frosty mug. He thanked her, and as he grabbed the glass, he tipped over the bottle with his arm.

Instinctively, Brenda reached for it and caught it just before its contents spilled all over the floor and her hand. The brown longneck was cold and wet with condensation, and the smell of beer slightly nauseated her, harking back to those few times in college when she had overindulged with her eventual husband.

"Ah, thanks," the older gentleman said, taking the bottle from her. "Wouldn't want to lose out on my last beer on Earth." A little giggle followed.

Brenda shook her head again with disgust. "How can you drink at a time like this? Oh yeah, you're already on the flight. I'll bet you're even in first class."

He took a substantial pull from his mug, licked his lips in satisfaction, and set it on the table. "Young lady, I realize you're upset," he said. "But have you considered the possibility that you're going about this all wrong?"

At that point, Sherman thought about his sweet Bess and all the wonderful times they'd had together, raising three children—Michael, Linda, and Amy— loving them, and loving each other. The best part of Sherman's day was when he arrived home from the plant and kissed his wife. Sure, there were tough times, like when the union went on strike and they had no money for two weeks and Michael's car accident in high school when he nearly died.

But love allowed them to persevere and focus on the moment.

Sounded like this woman's focus was always on the beyond, and Sherman said so.

She wrinkled her nose and looked at him as if he had two heads. "Well, of course," she spat. "The whole point of living on Earth is to serve the Lord and be His hands. If you do that, you'll get to Heaven. If you don't," and here she wagged her head back and forth, "there'll be consequences."

Sherman looked at his watch. It was 9:43 a.m. They would be boarding soon, and this woman looked as desperate as a quarterback with the pocket breaking down.

"I'm getting on that plane," she said with resolve. She stood and started weaving her way through the crowd past the loud college guys, who were apparently enjoying their drinks.

Sherman sighed. *It's going to be a long day and night and whatever for her*, he thought.

*****

Brenda was haranguing Roz, and the fact that the woman in the blue uniform was maintaining her cordial air was a testament to her professionalism. Even Brenda had to admit that deep down.

"I'm sorry, ma'am, we just don't have any room on this flight," Roz said after checking her computer monitor for the third time.

"But…" Brenda broke in.

"I'm very sorry, I wish there was something I could do."

"I have money. I can pay," Brenda said, thinking of the divorce settlement funds that she had tithed on, leaving a sizable chunk for a rainy day. And now, it was pouring.

A bit of a half-smile, half-grimace from Roz, as if to say, *You silly girl.*

"Ma'am, money doesn't exist here," she said simply. "And even if it did, I couldn't get you on. I'm really very sorry, but my hands are tied."

The tears came fast. Rivulets rolled down Brenda's cheeks, one entering the left corner of her mouth, which was hot and salty and oppressive. "This isn't fair. I followed the Bible and my pastor!" she blathered, drawing quiet stares from everyone else at the gate, all of whom were ready to board. They felt just as hot to Brenda as the tears rolling down her face. Roz nodded to someone, and moments later there was a gentle hand on Brenda's shoulder. She turned with both fervor and contempt.

An airport security officer. A large black man with a kind face in a navy polo shirt. "Come on, ma'am, let's go sit down and work all this out," he said, friendly enough but firmly. Plus, his hand remained on her shoulder.

"You don't understand," she said, now full-out crying, trying and failing to get control of her sniffles. "I have to get on this flight—it's as simple as that. I just don't know how I ended up on standby when I was so…"

Another voice behind her. Familiar. "She can have my seat."

Roz's eyebrows rose as Brenda whipped around.

It was the old man from Chili's.

***

Sherman couldn't run to the bathroom, much less run across the hallway to the gate. But he moved as quickly as he could, because it looked like the blonde woman was about to flip her lid. A security officer with bulging biceps had his hand on her shoulder. His partner, an equally large white man, hovered in the background, reassuring the travelers waiting to board the flight that everything was okay.

Maybe it was the beer, but the closer Sherman got to the podium, the more he knew what he had to do.

He loved Bess. She would understand. She'd be waiting.

"She can have my seat," he said as he arrived at the podium, out of breath. "Let her on the plane. It's clearly very important to her."

The woman from the airline adjusted the red scarf around her neck and gave Sherman a hard stare. "Are you sure you want to do this, sir?" she said. "I know there are loved ones waiting for you at your destination. It might be awhile until we can get you on another flight."

No hesitation. "I'm sure," he replied. "Let her go. I'll wait."

That's when he sensed Bess's presence and a release of sorts. Peace.

Everything, indeed, would be okay.

He started to respond, but the blonde woman cut him off.

"Thanks," she said, without a smile, "though it shouldn't have come to this. My pastor said…"

"Ma'am," the woman from the airline said evenly, and this time without a smile, "you're going to miss your flight if you don't hurry."

As the blonde woman took long strides toward the Jetway, almost running, Sherman couldn't resist the urge to shake his head just a little.

And was the woman from the airline doing the same?

***

Brenda boarded the aircraft and moved all the way to the rear, two rows from the back. Compared to other flights she had been on, it was relatively quick, because there were no overhead bins, nobody struggling to stuff an oversized carryon into an already crowded space. That always annoyed her, but now she was reminded of her lost pink tote. Her Bible had been in there, along with several spiral notebooks filled with scribblings from services and, of course, her multicolored highlighter pens. All gone.

An androgynous flight attendant with feathered hair and high cheekbones welcomed her and directed her to a window seat.

"Can I get you anything, ma'am?" he said in a pleasant, falsetto voice, almost like that of a choirboy. *He was probably gay*, Brenda thought. *No way he was in a choir. At least not at my church. I wonder if gay people get into Heaven.*

She shook her head no, and the flight attendant turned around to help another passenger, a young man in a New York Mets T-shirt.

Ding.

The pilot, a Captain Engel, greeted the passengers and said the flight would take roughly an hour and thirty minutes, perhaps ten or fifteen minutes sooner if the prevailing winds were favorable.

"We're going to turn the Fasten Seatbelt sign on, so we ask that you stay in your seats until we are airborne, and I'll let you know when you can safely move about the cabin," he said.

Brenda tapped her finger on her lap. *Come on, come on.*

A minute turned into five and then ten.

When are we leaving? Brenda thought, her heart just now starting to beat a little faster.

"Uh, folks, we're just about ready to depart, but we have some last-minute details to address, so give us a few minutes and we'll take off," Captain Engel said in a reassuring voice.

***

Sherman had found a seat within the gate area and sat down to catch his breath. At least he couldn't have another heart attack, probably.

In awhile, he would head back to Chili's and maybe order another beer. The Pabst had reminded him of the first one he'd ever had, on the back stoop with his own father when he was sixteen, about a year before he enlisted in the Army. Two years after that he had witnessed some of the worst carnage anyone could ever withstand at places like Tarawa and Iwo Jima.

He had been a wreck when he returned home, the sounds of shellfire echoing in his mind, but his Bess…his beautiful, loving, practical Bess…had calmed the devils.

Without her, there was no him. There was no Michael and Linda and Amy.

There was no love.

"Sir?" Sherman looked up. "Hi there, my name is Roz. I want to offer you a unique opportunity…"

***

Ten minutes became fifteen, and now Brenda was on the verge of panic. Was this whole altruistic, give-up-my seat thing just a put on? Were TSA agents going to come back and deplane her?

No. I won't allow it, she thought as she worked to make herself look smaller in her seat.

"Folks, the last few passengers have entered the aircraft, and we'll be closing the door and departing momentarily," Captain Engel's scratchy voice broke through. "Flight attendants, please take your seats and prepare for departure."

The takeoff was smooth, and the whitest light Brenda had ever seen bore through her window; it was so bright she slid down the shade. She tried dozing, but while the flight was smooth, thoughts danced around in the alcoves of her mind.

Her eternal reward was nigh, but it still nagged at her that it had taken a total stranger to get her to this point. It wasn't what she had done, which was, in her estimation, everything she could have. She had done everything she had been told by people like her pastor, Joyce Meyer, and every other guest preacher that came to her church.

No matter. She was on her way. And it was going to be glorious.

Those thoughts tumbled around her mind until she finally found rest.

The landing was so smooth she didn't awaken until Captain Engel said over cheers and clapping, "Well folks, we've arrived. We've opened the door, and you'll be debarking shortly. On behalf of myself and your flight crew, thanks for flying with us, and welcome to Heaven."

It took nearly ten minutes for Brenda to deplane, another annoyance, but when she stepped onto the Jetway, a warmth penetrated every crevice of her soul. That same light from when the plane took off was more intense now, almost too much, and she had to shield her eyes. The only respite came when she seemed to float up the Jetway tunnel and then into the presence of the light itself.

There, in front of it, was the old man in the embrace of a woman about his age, and they were becoming progressively younger as they kissed.

The thoughts firing away in Brenda's cerebral cortex kept coming back to the same thing: *How? How could the old man have made it on the plane? He gave up his seat, and by his own admission, he wasn't saved.*

Like a lot of things that had happened that morning, it just didn't see plausible.

There was a tap on her shoulder, and she turned to find a robust Hispanic man in a blue uniform with epaulettes and a gold badge. An ID card that showed his smiling face over his name, Juan, and the letters TSA hung from his right shirt collar.

But this man wasn't smiling.

"Ma'am, you need to come with me," he said, grabbing her by the arm while simultaneously reaching for the two-way radio attached to his belt buckle.

"This is Gonzalez. Over," he said into the radio with a brisk, businesslike tone, his pink lips near touching it. "We've got another stowaway."

A stowaway? Brenda's heart fluttered as she fumbled with this idea and then caught sight of the old man, now a young man with a shock of sandy-brown hair and upper-body muscles, maybe in his early twenties. He was dressed in a khaki military uniform, complete with a tie that was stuffed between the buttons of his shirt. The woman with him was about the same age and wore a flowered dress, a wide-brimmed sun hat, and white heels.

"I'm *not* a stowaway!" she blathered to the TSA agent before turning to the old man. "Sir? Sir! Tell him you gave up your seat so I could get on this flight! Tell him!"

Sherman held Bess's hand and shook his head. "Love," he said. "Love is all that mattered. That's where you missed it, my dear."

The burly TSA agent led the blonde woman away toward a dark alcove, where there was an ominous gray metal door.

The placard on the door simply read: "Holding Cell."

CAST FROM EDEN

Culberson County, Texas

The multicolored stones that comprised the church building's foundation were cool to the touch in the desert's crack of dawn and, in fact, made Raymond Diaz shiver slightly. Which did nothing to diminish the jackhammer chiseling away at his temples, but in his haze, he was able to appreciate the minute strain of relief.

Migraines were a bitch.

Hidden sin. That's what coarse language is, even when used in the mind or under the breath. *Hold it*, he thought, *hold it…* That's exactly what Pastor El is preaching about right now. *I may be on the outs with him, but he's got a point.*

Gotta stay clean, Raymond thought. *Gotta stay pure.*

The rhythm of pastor's voice floated down through the open window above him and kept time with the jackhammer. "Don't you see, church?" the high-pitched cadence of Pastor Eldridge Waldo Murphy III projected, as the West Texas sun was just beginning its oppressive march skyward toward Raymond Diaz. "Don't you see? "The enemy'll try every way possible to worm his way into your life, like we saw earlier with our brother, Raymond. But that's when you gotta repent of hidden sin, speak to your circumstances, and mix it with faith. Amen."

Raymond had tried that, or rather more accurately, *was* trying that. Under his ragged, sweat-soaked Texas Tech T-shirt, which provided scant protection from the sun, he was, in fact, screaming at his situation, commanding the devil to depart from him into dry, arid places, of which there were plenty in Culberson County. It was the faith part that still stymied him.

Hebrews 11:1: Faith is the substance of things hoped for, the evidence of things not seen.

Oh, my God—ah, gosh—it hurts.

Pastor El kept on: "The faithless, like our brother outside, are blind, stumbling along, bumping into walls and things. Praise God."

Which was a little funny—funny peculiar—because moments before, Raymond Diaz had stumbled from the rear of the church toward the pulpit while Pastor El was preaching. He had actually stopped the service as he bawled on his knees, asking the Lord for mercy and for the laying of hands to deliver him from the blinding pain that had plagued him after the Army's initial push to Baghdad as part of Operation Iraqi Freedom way back in '03.

"How dare thee interrupt the Lord's servant?" Pastor El thundered, then motioned toward male attendants lining either side of the pews—make that Holy Ghost benches—to physically remove him from the Church of Zoar. With long fingers squeezing his underarms, they escorted Raymond, legs dragging behind him, past congregants who looked as if they were tsk-tsking in their outdated suits and dresses.

The enormous oak door in the foyer swung open, and Raymond was hastily shoved into the dusty street to be alone with his reprobate mind. The mind that was trying like heck to surf the mammoth waves of lightning-bolt pain as the strains of "Nothing but the Blood of Jesus" began drifting out of the open windows, a tinny piano keeping time with fatigued voices trying hard to prove they were still excited about Jesus at 6:33 a.m. on the Lord's Day.

Miles to the west, an indigo cube emerged soundlessly from the murky dawn shadows; the abundant population of desert scrub and *javelina* bush seemed to bow to its presence as it passed overhead. Somewhere nearby, a jackrabbit paused to stare skyward, sniffing at the airborne intruder, then returning to its early morning foraging, ever mindful of predators.

Raymond Diaz had arrived at the steps of the Church of Zoar six months earlier after drifting down from the Mescalero Apache reservation near Almagordo, his tribal homeland between the four sacred mountains. The migraines had come with him, a byproduct of his service in Iraq, the rank tension brought on by IEDs and snipers and watching buddies become broken men, both physically and psychologically. According to Pastor El—in a tragic attempt at being perceived as hip in the eye's of the congregation's dozen or so bored children—his migraines were, in fact, caused by "demons doing the devil's work." Only copious amounts of prayer, speaking in tongues, and laying of hands would vanquish them.

What the hell? Raymond thought, perhaps blasphemously, of the Pentecostal treatment trifecta,

What have I got to lose? But it had worked. For a few months, the tornado of pain subsided after Raymond had dutifully raised his hands to the northernmost transom of the ramshackle church in praise to Him and fell backward into the arms of one of the attendants, slain in the Spirit.

From that point on, Raymond was a fixture at the Church of Zoar, and the handsome man with rough-hewn facial features and a thatch of black hair did everything he could to soak up the God's Word, sitting at the feet of Pastor El. He dutifully marked up his Bible with highlighter pens he had bought on a trip to Van Horn, the Culberson County seat, along with color-coded notebooks he'd filled to capacity with scribblings made during daily services. For the first time since before Iraq, it felt good to be alive. His six-foot gait had a little more pep, and he started dressing for church in his twenty-year-old blue suit and green tie, although they clashed. He also began tithing on his Army disability checks to ensure his ongoing relief.

But then, like little droplets of rain, the migraines returned with more force than ever. One recent Sunday morning, Raymond blacked out while sauntering up the church's cracked wooden steps, just as the service was beginning. His notebooks and Bible spilled onto the sandy ground, the pages fluttering open like so many leaves. That had drawn a crowd with Pastor El at its center, rebuking the devil and commanding the evil spirits to depart to arid places in the majestic "Name of Jesus." Pastor El had whipped himself into a fury something fierce; the beads of sweat coalesced on his brow and dripped into Raymond's eyes, a sting that resonated through the shockwave of pain he'd felt upon awakening.

Over time, Raymond came to church less often, trying other remedies, such as visiting the Beaumont Army Hospital in El Paso, where he was prescribed Tylenol with codeine. He even returned to the res to undergo a healing ritual, the long-forgotten chants of the medicine man flowed back to him like a familiar river. None of which worked, so he was forced to beg Pastor El to answer his question: "Why has God forsaken me?"

"I can't help you if you don't repent of the hidden sin in your life, Raymond," Pastor El answered quietly one morning in his spartan office at the rear of the Church of Zoar, a photo of a solemn Jesus stared heavenward. "Doesn't the Lord say it perfectly in Isaiah 30:15? 'In repentance and rest is your salvation.' The gospel of Matthew adds to it: 'Produce fruit in keeping with repentance.'

"The Lord's is trying to tell you something, Raymond. Are you listening? You might be *hearing* the words of his faithful servant, but are you really *listening* to them? Listening implies action toward an end goal."

That exhortation, spoken just weeks before being ejected from the church today, echoed in the rock-filled caverns of Raymond's mind as the cube silently made its way across the windswept plain. The cube was just that: a plain box with perfect equilateral lines. No windows, lights, or antennae indicated an intelligent presence. It had no markings, but in the emerging dawn's torturous light, minute grooves like layers might have been seen by anyone who could have gotten close enough.

Raymond peered up and saw something in the sky moving his way from the west; it didn't look like a plane, but seemed just as big and foreboding as a C-130. He assumed it was a hallucination because his migraines had fooled him before. He pulled the T-shirt tightly over his head to shut out the growing sunlight, screwed his eyes shut, and prayed:

"I am healed by the blood of Jesus.

I am healed by the blood of Jesus.

Forgive me of my hidden sin, Lord. I repent of sins of commission and omission.

I am healed by the blood of Jesus."

He looked again, and the cube was almost overhead. *What the hell…? Sorry, heck.*

There were subtle changes, too. For instance, the cube's corners were becoming ever so slightly rounded as minute bits of material began to fall, at first almost imperceptibly, but then, like an cloudburst, a pillar of dark snow fell in the early morning light.

A pillar. A few weeks before, Pastor El had preached about Lot's wife. "Y'wanna look back at your sin?" he had bellowed. "Y'wanna think about all the fun you had in the world, carousing and using the Lord's precious Name to curse and swear? Praise God, you do that, and I believe you'll suffer the same fate as Lot's wife. You don't wanna be a pillar of salt, do you?"

Nope.

The Church of Zoar had been established by Pastor El's grandfather, one of the original Azusa Street clan who took Brother Seymour's exhortation to make disciples of all nations literally. Church historiography indicates that a group of about seventy-five pilgrims departed the Azusa Street Pentecostal revival in Los Angeles in early 1909, intending to reach Haiti and evangelize the heathen of that nation.

But after an arduous journey via a convoy of early automobiles and horse-drawn wagons across the hellish Mojave Desert, Pastor El's grandfather had a revelation at the far eastern perimeter of Culberson County: "Here," he said, "is where the Lord commands me to build His church."

That church, the original building, was constructed in the winter of 1911. It eventually evolved into the unincorporated Town of Zoar, so named after the Biblical city God spared before destroying Sodom and Gomorrah and turning Lot's wife into a pillar of salt. The generations of true believers became the salt of the West Texas earth. Their path to the light was on their knees in the Church of Zoar, not to mention fair amounts of government assistance, especially during the Great Depression and the economic downturns of the early 1980s and, eventually, the late 2000s.

The Church of Zoar was an emulation of the biblical churches at Galatia, Corinth, Rome, and other places where St. Paul had written letters to gentile converts in the post-Christ Mediterranean world. That was, of course, after being knocked off his high horse by the Almighty on the road to Damascus. In his case, the sin was overt, not hidden.

"Imagine that, church," Pastor El proclaimed during a three-hour sermon on a Wednesday night months ago. "Our little God-serving community of Zoar, spoken of in the same breath as Rome, capital of It-ah-lee, with its Coliseum and frescoes and palaces. But that's what the Lord intended all along: one God and His church in every community, including ours. Amen."

It was difficult to discern where the *Church* of Zoar ended and where the *Town* of Zoar began. As the grandson of the founder, and thus a blood connection to the wonderment of Azusa Street, Pastor El was the unquestioned leader of the Zoar congregation. A church board of elders was comprised of his children and a few other lifelong church members who could trace their lineage back to the Great Revival in Los Angeles. The board of elders, led by Pastor El, also doubled as the town's secular leadership, controlling all commercial and legal decisions. That included the occasional casting out of a citizen who had made a foolhardy decision, for example, to steal from the common food supply because their children were hungry.

That also included the removal of people like Raymond Diaz, whose clear lack of faith was the work of the evil one and could become a virus that might, ultimately, bring both church and town to ruin. The board of elders met at Pastor El's two-story parsonage every Monday night after service for dinner and discussion of church and town affairs. Tomorrow, that is where a decision about Raymond Diaz's future would be decided.

This morning, however, Raymond peered out from under his T-shirt and expected to see the indigo cube resting in the sky, perhaps a few hundred feet in the air. But it was visibly smaller than it had been fifteen minutes earlier; the amount of its falling material had found its way onto the dusty surface of the Town of Zoar, its ragtime-era buildings now feeling the brunt of an otherworldly source.

And then something new. A generous chunk of material—Raymond thought it looked like a conglomerate of seeds—had bounced and rolled within about ten feet of him. The material burrowed its way into the grimy, unpaved street in front of the church, and moments later, verdant shoots of vines began protruding from the soil and growing at a tremendous rate.

It killed him to move because the jackhammer in his head suddenly became a sledgehammer. But since he clearly wasn't hallucinating, Raymond forced himself to spider crawl over the newly sprouted vines and touch them. They were cool and throbbed as if living beings with a pulse, and they smelled earthy, like the odor of a forest after an early morning rain. Kneeling now, he surveyed the town square and noticed the vegetation was beginning to look like a soft carpet of grass. Across the square, Pastor El's two-story parsonage, with its turreted, pillared porch, now had vines growing through its slats. A dark-stained rocking chair was consumed by three thin vines, and Raymond could hear its tender legs cracking under the strain.

Whatever it was, it was going after the Church of Zoar.

Raymond stood and turned to face the church, where the strains of "Rock of Ages" floated across the town square, juxtaposing with the vines that began creeping up the sides of the building. One thin, snake-like protrusion had wrapped itself around the spire and wiggled the cross at its summit until it fell, bouncing once off the roof and then onto the street.

Feeling a tug at his ankle, Raymond looked down with macabre interest as a particularly aggressive vine began to wrap itself around his Army-issued right combat boot and the hem of his black jeans. He quickly pulled his leg away and dashed across the town square, past the gaudy wooden cross at its center, sans the figure of a crucified Jesus. Which was "a Big C thing, a Catholic thing" Pastor El had said. "They still got Him on that cross, but we got *real* church here in Zoar, not some dead religion.

"We got the God that saves!"

And everybody said, "Amen!"

The most important thing that had ever happened to both church and town was the 1933 weeklong visit of the world's most renowned evangelist, Aimee Semple McPherson. Sister Aimee had responded to a formal invitation from Pastor El's grandfather and made her way across the desert in her grand, green, four-door Cadillac convertible, a gift from her Foursquare Church congregation in Los Angeles.

The services, Raymond had often heard from the pulpit, were legendary: long swaths of scripture complemented by great gusts of tongues, the incoherent babble seamlessly becoming applause as Sister Aimee exhorted her new charges well into the night. At the conclusion of her visit, she posed for a photograph with the pastor's family. That portrait hangs in the parlor of Pastor El's parsonage, but Raymond had never seen it. He had been told about it plenty of times, though.

Suddenly, a vine crashed through the stained-glass window that fronted the home's parlor, and for a fleeting second, Raymond considered saving the portrait. *But that's crazy,* he thought, pushing the thought out of his mind.

Instead, he bounded up the church steps and nearly tripped over a fat, wayward vine that had sprouted leaves that were turning into their own vines. He tried to pull open the solid oak door, but didn't quite catch the faded brass handle the first time. He tried again and used the last vestiges of his military strength training to slam it to the side with a boom that compelled much of the faithful to turn in his direction.

Pastor El was in front of the pulpit, laying hands on the corpulent Earnestine Rhone, who had battled diabetes for as long as Raymond had been in Zoar.

"I *rebuke* you, Satan!" he shrieked at the top of his lungs, using both of his hands to cup Earnestine's flabby neck; the congregants murmured their agreement and held out their hands toward them. Her eyes were closed, her lips moving in silent acquiescence. "I *command* you to depart from this woman in Jesus's mighty Name! You are *not* welcome in the Lord's house, praise God!"

The sanctuary had become slightly darker as the vines outside began to crowd the stained-glass windows that were exactly the same as those in Pastor El's parsonage. Raymond raced to the apse and raised his hands in front of Pastor El, now in the throes of tongues as Earnestine fell backward into the arms of an attendant who had magically appeared.

"Ah-LA-LA-LA-cashuma-lo-lo-LA-kolasha-eh-LA-puntemen…"

"Pastor! Pastor!" Raymond interrupted. "You have to see… Come outside. Quickly!"

With his toast-colored hair and paunch nearly obscuring his belt, Pastor El kept right on going, apparently doused in the Holy Spirit: "… Tresheman-LA-LA-otumoman-lo-LA-LA-cashuma…"

Raymond grabbed the pastor's right arm with both of his and shook him enough to get him to stumble toward the first of three steps leading to the pulpit. It broke the spell.

"You are *not* welcome in my church to grieve the Spirit of God!" Pastor El roared at Raymond, smoothing the slightly wrinkled fabric of his charcoal three-piece suit that would have been worthy of Wall Street. "I command thee to get behind me, Satan—you are not welcome in this…"

"Will you listen? There's something outside, and it's dissolving into stuff that's growing into vines. Look!" Raymond spluttered, and he turned and pointed to the windows. By now the reds and blues and purples of the stained glass were much darker, darker even than when Zoar was covered by infrequent storm clouds. But then, and now, no one seemed to care as the church's praise-and-worship leader Charlie Smith's piano swung into "Down to the River to Pray":

"O sisters, let's go down,

Let's go down, come on down

O sisters, let's go down

Down in the river to pray."

Earnestine Rhone, still lying prone on the carpet, had opened her eyes just barely and shifted her head toward the nearest window. Her eyes grew wide, but then darted to Pastor El, who was now standing over her, pointing his forefinger at her. "You focus on the Lord, Earnestine!" he admonished. "You focus on Him who's healed you!" As almost an afterthought, he added: "You focus on Hebrews: 'Therefore, He is able to save completely those who come to God through Him!' 'Completely' means anything, Earnestine. Anything! Even the specter lying in wait outside your tent."

At the same time, Raymond realized his migraine had dissipated and then disappeared completely. *Probably the adrenalin,* he thought, although when a migraine ceased, there were always aftershocks, like an earthquake. He kept waiting for one as he stood next to the pulpit while a livid Pastor El pointed a fat index finger at him. But nothing. It was as if he had been reborn. *Born again.*

Can it be the cube? Raymond thought. *Does it have some kind of otherworldly healing power?*

Where did it come from? Why was it attacking the Church of Zoar? And why did he feel, physically, so…good?

Without warning, a monstrous vine, roughly two feet in diameter, crashed through the roof of the church, causing a gaping hole and showering the faithful with wood chips and dust, lots and lots of dust.

A ripple of gasps swept through the congregation, and a very few turned toward the center aisle, waiting for someone, anyone to make the first move to the large oaken doors in the rear. But Pastor El jumped over Earnestine Rhone, who by now was desperately trying to get to her feet as another vine broke through the stained-glass window closest to her.

"Don't go! Don't go!" Pastor El shouted at the top of his lungs. "Jesus saves, and He will save us from this calamity. Remember Job! 'Yet does not one in a heap of ruins stretch out his hand, or in his disaster therefore cry out for help?'"

"Forget this," Raymond shouted as he ran down the center aisle to the doors, which had begun to bow slightly due to external pressure. Behind Raymond, several people followed, dodging others who were kneeling, praying in tongues, and raising their hands toward the roof, where the large vine had sprouted subordinate vines. They reminded Raymond of his grammar school English classes on the res, where he learned about the Greek myth of Medusa the Gorgon and the venomous snakes that made up her hair.

He reached the doors, but couldn't push them open, so he backed up and rammed one with his shoulder. It budged, and he was able to stick his foot through just enough to hold it back from the onslaught of the crowding vegetation outside.

"Move! Move!" he admonished the dozen or so congregants behind him. He gave the doors one final ram with his right shoulder, which allowed them to escape one by one. Before leaving, he glanced down the center aisle in time to see a large vine wrap itself around Pastor El, whose arms were stretched out like Jesus on the cross. A hefty beam crashed down from the ceiling, knocked him over, and pinned him to the floor. More dust from the fallen beam made it seem the Church of Zoar was filled with smoke.

Somewhere, he heard the chant waft over the commotion: "Jesus saves. Jesus saves. Jesus saves." Chaos reigned as people had mere seconds to contemplate their choice: faith or fear.

Outside, the town square was essentially a greenhouse. The cross in the center of the square was down, and Pastor El's parsonage had caved in. The general store was all but destroyed, yet he could still see the far peaks of the Guadalupe Mountains in the distance, one of his tribe's sacred places.

Raymond had loved playing video games as a kid, and every birthday he was allowed to go to the mall in Alamogordo to play in its arcade. His particular favorite was Gorf, with its robotic voice that said, "There is no…escape, Space…Cadet."

Instead of the migraine, those words echoed through his mind as he sought a means of escape, since the town was perhaps reaping the rewards of its own hidden sins.

Through a break in the vegetation, he found a possibility. It was the Church of Zoar's 1970s-era beater school bus, complete with the church motto, *Excited About Jesus,* painted in blocky, indigo letters on the side. The decrepit diesel monster was used to haul the faithful to revival meetings in El Paso, Odessa, and Midland, and once it had been used to travel all the way to Lubbock for a healing service hosted by Benny Hinn himself at Texas Tech's basketball arena. Raymond had been on that trip that took on a decidedly more serious tenor when the bus ran out of fuel just east of Pecos. While Pastor El and the other pilgrims had been begging God for deliverance on their knees on the side of Interstate 20, he had flagged down a Texas state trooper, and they refueled in Pecos. That's when Raymond had learned to drive a school bus, a skill he never thought he'd use again.

But the opportunity to escape the cacophony of creeping vegetation was there if Raymond and the other escapees could survive a trip across the town square. By now the cube was nearly dissolved, merely a black dot in the sky. Raymond used what was left as a point of reference as he led his followers first along the side of the church, then over, under, and around the vines, hustling over a lush carpet of grass that covered the ground.

After a thunderous crash, Raymond turned to find the Church of Zoar completely gone with nothing but miles of desert beyond. He could barely hear what was left of the frightened voices within silenced as the bell tower tipped over. Nearby,

Charlie Smith screamed for help as a vine wrapped itself around his neck, causing his eyes to bulge out of their sockets and his tongue to protrude from his mouth, gasping for air. He fell, and was swallowed by the vines.

The group had made its way around the perimeter of town past several demolished homes and reached the apparent edge of the vegetation, which abruptly came to an end like recently laid sod. The bus was about twenty feet away, and Raymond Diaz hoped like hell the keys were in their usual spot, the ignition. It wasn't as if Zoar was a high-crime community. His heart sank when he arrived at the door and they weren't there. He shoved open the door with both hands, nearly gagged at the pungent, sour odor, then knelt in the cracked leather of the green driver's seat and felt around the sun visor for the key. Nope. Then it dawned on him that Pastor El must have had the bus keys on his keychain, along with keys to just about every other building in town, including the general store, most of the homes, and, of course, the church. He was funny that way.

The group milling outside the bus, now eleven total, fidgeted and observed the oncoming vegetation with increasing angst, while three vines as thick as tree trunks flattened what remained of the general store in what almost appeared to be a coordinated attack, leaving just the cinder block foundation. Eight climbed aboard the bus, taking seats that faced the carnage, while the remaining three knelt in a makeshift prayer circle outside the bus's door.

"My God, my God, why have You forsaken us?" bleated Rebecca Schauer, perhaps the best-looking woman in Zoar, Raymond reckoned. She was a twenty-five year old with a lithe, gymnast's body and long, straight amber hair and opaline eyes. It was true that Raymond harbored a secret lust for Rebecca; maybe that was the hidden sin to which Pastor El had been alluding.

But he quickly dismissed the thought as he determined to start the bus without the key. Amid the terrible sound of wood and other building materials straining, and then snapping and collapsing against the sheer weight of the vegetation, Raymond peered under the dash. There was a rat's nest of multicolored wires coated with at least four decades of dust and soot, and while Raymond had a rudimentary knowledge of electrical relays and terminals from his time in the Army, there was no way he would be able to figure out how to hotwire the bus in a matter of seconds.

Seemingly beaten, Raymond rolled over, bumped his head against the base of the seat, and cursed loudly. Then he saw something silvery in his peripheral vision—an ancient piece of duct tape, corners pealing and an oblong indentation in the middle. He yanked the lower left corner and the tape gave way, the adhesive pulling like pizza cheese. Raymond pulled the welcome key off. It was cool to the touch and sticky; who knew how long the spare had been there?

Hopping into the driver's seat, he inserted the key into the ignition and turned it; the engine coughed for several seconds before dying. *Damn,* Raymond thought, but Rebecca and the others were still kneeling and babbling in tongues as smaller vines began to consume the empty ground around them.

Raymond tried again, and this time the engine turned over reluctantly, barely idling. *Hot dog*, he thought.

"Come on, people, let's go!" Rebecca and the other congregants quickly boarded the bus, while he depressed the clutch pedal and threw the stick shift into first gear. Balding tires could be heard crunching the ground as the bus ambled forward inch by inch before gaining speed, rolling over desert scrub as it made for Nevel Road on the south side of the little that was left of Zoar.

Reaching the road, Raymond headed east into the rising sun, the horizon orange and billowy with cumulus clouds. Assuming the rampaging vegetation was in pursuit, he shifted gears—second, third, fourth, and finally fifth as he pushed the bus to 50 mph—perhaps its maximum speed considering its elder status. It took about twenty minutes to reach the green highway sign that indicated the Reeves County line, when a loud bang from underneath the hood shuddered the bus, followed by gray thicket of smoke. The bus coasted for about a mile and then came to a complete stop, straddling the road's divided yellow line. A hawk circled overhead, then darted south toward the US-Mexico border.

Zoar was no longer visible from the road, although a plume of thin, fine dust had risen in the air like a pillar, the last vestige of the terrific metamorphosis the town had undergone. Raymond's heart, which had been visibly beating through his ragged Texas Tech T-shirt, a souvenir from his visit to the Lubbock revival months before, finally had slowed enough for him to catch his breath. He leaned back in the driver's seat, closed his eyes, and realized once again that his migraine had vanished. Maybe the indigo cube had healing powers and had done what Pastor El and his laying of hands had been unable to accomplish. Raymond didn't know. All he felt was a distracting wave of relief.

"Come on, let's go," he finally said to the faithful, whose faith had seemingly been shaken as they huddled together in the back three or four seats of the bus. One by one they trooped to the exit, disembarked, and gathered in a group that stared at Raymond, their de facto leader. They said nothing, behaving like sheep at the shearer.

"Well, what do you think we should do?" Raymond asked, annoyed, and took a few steps eastward down the road, which had become Brooks Pecos Road somewhere along their escape from Zoar. When no one answered, he said, "Let's walk. There's a town about five miles from here, I think. The sun will be overhead soon, and we can't afford to be out here when that happens. You wanna bake?"

He got about ten feet down the road when he realized no steps were coming up behind him. He turned, and the faces of the faithful were illuminated by the rising sun, but were devoid of emotion, as if their moral mooring had been severed, and they were trying desperately to make some sense of it all.

Raymond contemplated saying something, anything to motivate them, but he simply didn't have the words. They were adults, but they were also children who had been told what to do by Pastor El for most of their lives. At some point, they had to grow up; now was as good a time as any. It occurred to him that they probably weren't going to make it in the great big world, even if they did survive their voyage through the desert.

So he turned eastward along the road and began walking again. He knew there was a town ahead, but truthfully, he wasn't sure if it was five miles or even ten, and he couldn't even remember the name. The only time he'd left Zoar on the bus for revivals was on Interstate 20 to the south. He layered over that his recollection of a news story he had seen on TV before his Iraq deployment about two inmates from an Arizona prison who had managed to escape and then died of exposure and dehydration just a few miles from the clink. He had chuckled to himself at the time. *Idiots*, he'd thought, but now it was no joke.

It didn't take Raymond Diaz long in Iraq to realize that mirages weren't hallucinations, they were optical illusions. One of the medics said it had something to do with the way light is bent, or refracted, by hot and cold temperatures. Thus, a refracted image of the sky on the ground can look like a cool, calm pool of life-giving water. There weren't any physics classes on the res—heck, they barely offered basic science classes—so that was all new to him. But worth remembering, as the Culberson County sun was getting to be as oppressive as it was overseas.

Left foot, right foot, breathe, he told himself as he made his way down the road. Just like Iraq, though back then he was toting fifty-plus pounds of equipment, a full camelback, an M-16, and a camouflaged helmet that had felt like an anchor on his head. After a mile or so, he looked back and realized he was alone; the bus's thick gray smoke was barely visible. The faithful had apparently decided to take their chances. Maybe there was some sense in that, as the bus provided at least some cover, but then again, someone would have to find them. The Culberson County sheriff's office was fifty miles away in Van Horn, and the white-and-green sheriff's cruiser only occasionally passed through the town. Zoar had the reputation of a peaceful, if peculiar, community that had little use for a police force thanks to the order kept by its domineering church leader. And a state trooper? Never.

To both the left and the right were miles and miles of desert, and for one brief, terrifying moment Raymond considered the possibility of a coyote attack, but dismissed it, reasoning coyotes were primarily nocturnal animals and would probably already be back in their dens to avoid the oncoming heat of the day.

As he trudged along, his mind continued to drift back to his early days at church and his Bible studies. *Commit to the Lord whatever you do*, he thought, and *your plans will succeed*. That was Proverbs 16:3. *And by fear of the Lord one keeps away from evil*. Proverbs 16:6. *The righteous cry out, and the Lord hears them, he delivers them from all their troubles*. Psalms, he seemed to recall, maybe Chapter 33 or 34? He couldn't remember the specific verse, but suffice to say, he was in a real position to literally cry out to the Lord, just like Rebecca Schauer and her faithful comrades, now a few miles away, had.

It wasn't as if Raymond had backslid, nor was he a "mental assenter," which Pastor El had said was worse. No, it was simple: He was perplexed by the fact that his migraines had disappeared for a season, but then returned with more virulence, enough to get him to consider, just briefly, ending it all. But that was too convenient, a permanent solution to what he surmised was a temporary problem. *Hell*, he thought, *I'd never had so much as a hangnail before Iraq. Besides, no one can be 100% certain what's on the other side.* What he wanted to avoid was the stark realization that he had made an eternal mistake. The Big C was clear on that point.

However, he'd been delivered from his migraines this morning, and hadn't he prayed for years for just that? Even in his darkest places, he had never really given up hope, though his faith had been shaken to its foundation. His big question had always been more of an indictment: Where was God?

As if on cue, a dark shape began to form through the heat-wave distortion on the left side of the road. It was a few miles off, but immediately Raymond could tell it was a building of some sort. Breaking into a slight run, Raymond thought better of it and slowed; no point expending the energy and risking dehydration, something he learned in Iraq. No, slow and steady, not to mention extreme vigilance, was the order of the day back then, as it was right now. He'd get there, and then he would be responsible for saving the faithful, including Rebecca Schauer.

Check that. God would be responsible for the saving. Raymond was merely the instrument. He praised Him who delivers the weak and the weary from harm. And for the first time in weeks Raymond's belief was sincere.

Twenty minutes later, with the sun now a burning lemon disk riding high in the sky, he reached the building: Restoration Community Church of Wayne City, Pastor Brendan Joyce presiding. Wayne City was the closest town. Its church was a modern brown-brick structure with ceiling-to-floor plate-glass windows, black soffit fascia, and a half-circle driveway where several late-model sedans were parked. No bell tower, but a brass cross adorned the left entrance door. No Jesus to be found.

He could faintly hear an electric guitar hitting the solo on one of those new Gospel tunes he had heard in Lubbock, "People Like Us," about which Pastor El had been both ambivalent and reticent. "Gimme them old-time hymns," he used to say. And Charlie Smith would oblige.

Raymond Diaz entered Restoration Community Church, a blast of air conditioning punching his face. He nearly fell to his knees in the foyer due to the rapid change in temperature, but was caught by a pair of ushers wearing indigo blazers, their lily-white nametags, like the church itself, new and gleaming. They sat him down on a wooden bench outside of the sanctuary, where presumably Pastor Joyce was stepping to the pulpit amid hoots and hollers not much different than in the Church of Zoar.

Remembering the faithful back in the bus, including (and especially) Rebecca, Raymond made himself rise and ran into the sanctuary and up to the clear plastic lectern, where a sharply dressed man of about thirty, curly blonde hair parted left to right and a microphone in his right hand was adjusting his notes. "Well, hello there, brother," he said with a kindly grin. "Who might you be?"

"Pastor…Church of Zoar…destroyed by something," Raymond stammered, finally out of breath. "Need help…"

This time, Raymond fell to his knees on the taupe carpet, eliciting an *Ohhh* from the congregation. Pastor Joyce darted around the lectern, the smile replaced by a grim countenance as the same two ushers grabbed his arms.

"Now, brother, just rest yourself," Pastor Joyce said, placing his hands on Raymond's forehead. "You're in a safe place now. The Lord is present here."

Outside, in the distance to the west, a small dot began to emerge, eventually evolving into the shape of a cube. It was soundless as it sauntered across the sky toward Restoration Community Church in Wayne City, Texas.

SUPER DOPPLER 12

Outside of Rapid City, South Dakota

A low rumble and then a double-flash of lightning so bright as if announcing the arrival of the devil. And then the devil himself arrived, cracking his leather whip so violently it made the trailer shake.

Jenn and Armando's wedding photo, the one in the sterling silver frame with the engraved date—Saturday, June 13, 2014—vibrated atop the ancient hardwood coffee table, an antique she had thought was kind of cute when they were living together in the apartment in town.

Before Armando had gotten deployed.

Before he was killed by something called an IED in someplace called Kandahar.

Before she ended up here with Kylie, who was sleeping in the "room" at the far end of the trailer they shared. Didn't matter how rainy it got, or hot or cold, she'd sleep through the night. She had been a wedding-night baby and had always been like that, thank God. She was four now, and kindergarten was within spitting distance, as Armando used to say.

Armando. Her bae. Why had he taken that second tour in Afghanistan?

"Babe, I have to," he had said matter-of-factly in the kitchen of their apartment on St. Patrick Street as he prepared enchiladas on the stove with his mother's homemade (and secret) sauce recipe.

"These guys, the Taliban, they're dangerous," he said, sprinkling Chihuahua cheese on the enchiladas. "They're like…," and he stepped back, sweeping his tongs in the air, "cockroaches, and their only goal is to retake the entire country and destabilize the whole region. They've got to be stopped, and who better to do that than your Rambo?"

He smiled that winning Hispanic smile, and she shook her head.

Half an hour later, after grandma had picked up Kylie for a trip to Robbinsdale Park and McDonald's for a Happy Meal, they were in bed. As the winds of ecstasy blew over her naked body, she allowed herself the notion of Child #2. But that didn't happen.

That had been six months ago. God, it felt like years.

***

"This is a live view downtown," the TV weatherman piped in, "and we haven't seen rain this heavy in years. If we look at the image from Super Doppler 12… See this red splotch here west of town?"

That's where Jenn and Kylie were. And as if a response: "If you're there, stay indoors, and don't try to go anywhere. The heart of this cell will pass in about, oh, let's say an hour or so, but until then you'll have to contend with…"

The compact flat-screen TV, a wedding gift from Armando's parents, blinked out.

Damn satellite dish. Always going down when something important is going on.

She picked up her iPhone. No service.

She couldn't go anywhere or even make a call. *Great*. The raindrops were a thousand pinpricks on the metal roof of the trailer.

The weatherman hadn't said anything about funnel clouds or tornadoes, but weren't they attracted to trailer parks somehow? She pushed that thought out of her mind and turned to walk the twenty feet to the back of the trailer to check on Kylie. May as well. There was nothing else to do. Another flash of lightning, but before the next whip crack, something else.

A rapping at the door.

Jenn froze in place, stared at the door, and then looked down the hallway toward Kylie's room. The cops, maybe checking on people?

My mother? God, please don't let it be my mother. She was a wonderful woman but sometimes a little tone deaf to things that could put her in danger.

Another loud rap. Whoever it was, they weren't going away.

She slumped into the couch and pulled her knees up to her chin, hoping for the best, but the rapping continued until a voice filtered through the cracks in the doorway. "Please," it said. "Please. I'm hurt. Please open up!"

Jenn pulled her knees closer to her chin and opened her eyes as wide as they would go, so much so that she eventually had to squint to relieve the strain. A long flash of lightning filled the room, illuminating the wedding picture, the faces happily gazing into the future Jenn was now living. Instead of a loud, unexpected crack, the thunder was low and deep—like how James Earl Jones would sound if he ever took up that line of work. For a moment, she imagined Mr. Jones's features as an addition to the faces on Mount Rushmore.

More knocking. "Please...I'm bleeding."

Blood. Jenn hated blood. She flinched at the sight of it when Kylie fell off her bike, the sticky red stuff dripping down her elbow, the crying doing absolutely nothing to assuage the nausea she felt. At that moment, she wondered if Armando had bled when he had been killed by the IED in Kandahar, Afghanistan, on the other side of the world. A fight someone else should have taken up. In fact, why was the U.S. even there to begin with?

Oh, right. The Taliban. The cockroaches.

Armando bleeding, gripping sand as the mountains in the distance glowered. Perhaps the guy who placed the bomb laughing nearby at the stupid infidel American who deserved to die for wreaking havoc in his country.

Armando bleeding. Calling out for Jenn, for Kylie. Crying.

Bleeding.

More knocking.

Maybe it's another vet, she thought, running multiple scenarios through her mind. *Sure, another vet who had somehow gotten caught in the storm, someone Armando knew. Probably crashed his car and cut himself up but good.* Jenn didn't know if they had storms like this in Afghanistan. Armando used to say that the country reminded him of Durango, where his family was from in Mexico. Rocky country that was, in its own way, beautiful, the blue sky mating on the horizon with the hills and sand beneath it, *javelina* brush sweeping away the clouds until the sun came down in full force, beating the backs of those, like his parents and grandparents, who were scratching to make a living.

Knock-knock-knock.

A pause, then more knocking.

Jenn considered telling the voice to go away, but then it would be obvious the trailer was occupied. Right now, maybe it wasn't. For all this voice knew, Jenn and Kylie—Kylie, her precious cargo—were in town because who in their right mind would choose to stay in a trailer park during a storm of this magnitude?

The wind swept up the rain and seemed to hurl it at the side of the trailer, making it shake, and Jenn cringed, not so much for her safety, but for that of the voice. What if it was a vet? Or maybe it was Mr. Braun from down the road, the nice hippie-ish older gentleman with the stark gray ponytail and sleeveless shirts with faded tattoos of the names of his two wives, one on each shoulder. That was bad luck, she was told. Kylie once asked him why he combed his hair like a girl, and he just laughed and laughed.

"I comb my hair this way because I am a girl," he said, touching her chin with his thumb and forefinger.

Kylie, who had been three at the time, scrunched up her nose in confusion.

That was after Armando had been deployed, but before he had gotten killed.

Mr. Braun was at the backdoor!

No he wasn't. The voice sounded younger and less husky than Mr. Braun's, though it was undoubtedly male. She had been sure of that all along.

"Please…please, can you help me? I don't want to die tonight."

Jenn placed her bare feet on the throw rug in front of the couch, the shag fabric feeling worn as the flat screen stared blankly into space. Was she really going to open the door of this rickety trailer, the only place she could afford after Armando, to a total stranger who had no business being out on a night like tonight?

No. Not a chance.

In response, the sky cracked again, and a dog howled somewhere in the distance.

Probably Cherokee, Mr. Braun's long-hair, black-and-white mutt, the friendliest dog Jenn had ever met. The first thing he did when he met three-year-old Kylie was lick her cheeks, which made her laugh loud and long. Made Mr. Braun laugh, too, before he scooped up Kylie in his arms and tickled her tummy, while the presidents on Mount Rushmore looked stately in the distance. It was the first time Jenn had smiled since moving into the trailer. The Army had just buried Armando in Pine Lawn out near Route 16 and had handed her a tricorner flag. Twenty-one-gun salute, the whole deal.

The thing with Cherokee was he hardly ever barked, which is why Kylie was so fond of him. Sure, if someone he didn't know stopped over, he might utter a token bark and then go back to his bed to sleep it off. Only once had Jenn seen him growl, at a scruffy kid wearing a black heavy-metal T-shirt (Slayer, maybe, or was it Iron Maiden?) who rang Mr. Braun's doorbell. Cherokee was roaming out front—Jenn had never seen him on a leash—and he clearly didn't like the kid. Mr. Braun came out of the house, shushed Cherokee, gave the kid a soul handshake, and invited him in, telling her and Kylie he would be out in a jiff, and he was. The kid got into a black Camaro and drove off toward I44, which led back into town.

But before leaving, he and Jenn had made eye contact, and those cold ocean-blue eyes. Wow. Almost seemed out of place on a punk like that. Guilt poured over her like hot lava.

Armando's dead, she thought. *What does that really mean?*

But that was it. And now Cherokee was barking and even made a mournful howl at one point before quieting down.

Why was Cherokee even outside in this weather?

Another knock. "Please, I know you're in there. Your name is Jenn, right? Jenn, you've gotta give me a hand. I'm not gonna make it." And then, "Your friend down the road is dead. I tried to save him, but I couldn't."

The first thing that came to Jenn's mind was Mr. Braun in the same wooden casket as Armando, with a decorated soldier saluting nearby. Mr. Braun had served, maybe in Vietnam, because he's mentioned someplace called Khe Sanh once before lighting a cigarette and quickly putting it out because Kylie was nearby, chasing Cherokee. He had a tattoo on his right arm that said MACV-SOG, whatever that meant. It looked military and had a skull with a beret and two knives crossed behind it.

The wind whipped the side of the trailer with a bucket of rain and even made it shake a bit, which made Jenn wonder if Kylie was awake.

He knew her name.

Mr. Braun, dead? *Dead?*

He knew her name.

The doorknob was cold to the touch, and Jenn had forgotten it was locked. Before turning the lock, she tried looking out the window, but couldn't see anything, even when lightning lit up the valley for a second or two.

Knock-knock.

Who's there?

Jenn took a deep breath and opened the door.

He was sitting on the wooden steps in a fetal-like position: his head down, one arm reaching around his legs, with the other tucked under his knees that touched his prominent chin. No shirt, and his jeans were torn, making him look naked at first glance.

Jenn had seen naked men before, of course, but not since Armando. It soiled her a bit, probably because the man clearly had a nice bod, muscular arms, and a mop top that was longish, but not too long.

It was the scruffy kid, the one Cherokee had growled at earlier.

She couldn't see his face, but she quickly dismissed the thought of his blue eyes. Those were yummy.

But he was indeed injured; a scarlet wound snaked up his tucked left arm, the rain washing away the blood that still flowed. Jenn had once harbored the notion of a nursing degree, which Armando had fully supported, and even took a few courses at

Western Dakota Tech. But that ended when she saw a PowerPoint presentation with graphic photos of traumatic injuries, one of them of a stabbing victim who had ultimately died. She finished the course, got a C, and then promptly dropped out. Armando supported that decision as well.

"Babe, you do what you want," he had said. "School's not for everyone. Nursing's not for everyone. You don't have to work. We can make it."

That made her love him the teensiest bit more, if that was possible. This was late in the evening, and ten minutes later, she was riding him, grinding her hips as they simultaneously climaxed. She was hoping for Child #2.

Didn't happen.

***

Jenn stood there at the screen door, and at first, the kid didn't move, but then he gradually turned his head toward her.

No car, though. *How had he gotten here?* she thought. *Walked?* That was probably suicidal in this weather.

She cracked the screen door, and he rocked himself forward and back. "You're gonna have to help me," he said, hand now over the wound and blood flowing through his fingers. "I'm cut but good, Jenn."

She swung open the door a bit more, careful not to smack the kid with it, and held it with her leg.

The rain felt cold, and her foot immediately became immersed in both rain and his blood, and the thought of HIV danced around in the back of her mind. Should have thrown on her Crocs. What would happen to Kylie if she got sick and would never recover? Poor people couldn't afford the drug cocktail that supposedly rid Magic Johnson of his HIV case, the one she learned about at Western Dakota Tech before she was compelled to drop out.

No. This was a kid. Maybe he was in a car accident. Yeah. That's why he didn't have his car.

But why isn't he wearing a shirt? A fire, maybe? In this rain?

"Can you support yourself?" she asked, as she helped the kid hobble onto the green shag rug. "I want to grab a towel and my first aid kit."

"I think so," he replied, then winced, and appeared to grip his arm even tighter.

"Don't touch it," Jenn implored, then turned and tiptoed toward the rear of the trailer, where her open-concept room was located, next to the closet bathroom that wasn't much bigger than one on an aircraft. At first she couldn't find the first aid kit, but then she remembered she'd shoved it under her bed when they moved in. She had to strain her arm to reach it, but she finally grabbed the handle of the blue box that had a white sticker with a red cross on the front. On her way out the door, she grabbed a clean, pink terry-cloth bath towel and a red bandanna she had casually thrown on the bed earlier that day.

The boy's back was turned to her as she arrived in the trailer's spartan living area. On his right shoulder blade was a red tattoo of an anarchy sign, the *A* slightly cocked to the left. His shoulder-length persimmon hair was straight, and rain water snaked its way down his back toward his butt crack.

Drop by drop blood dripped from the kid's wound onto the rug, creating a few half-dollar-sized, black-red pools. *I never liked it anyway*, Jenn thought. Armando had picked it up for a dollar at the Goodwill, and for the few years they lived in the apartment, it was stationed inside the doorway to absorb the snow from everyone's boots.

"Here, let me help you. I was training to be a nurse," Jenn said, kneeling down, dabbing the wound with the bath towel, which elicited an "Aaugh!" that she thought might be loud enough to wake up Kylie. The blood flow seemed to be slowing, and with that realization, she took up the bandanna and wrapped it around his leg to put pressure on the wound. Then she grabbed the orange-and-green afghan, a Christmas gift from Mom that was positioned over the seat back of the couch; she covered him with it and helped him settle into the couch. She hoped the blood wouldn't soak through the bandanna and into the couch's fabric, but what else could she do? He was hurt and needed to take a load off, because who knew how long it would take the paramedics to get there without phone service.

Jenn opened a folding chair nestled in the far corner and sat down. There was silence for a moment before the kid spoke: "Thanks," he said. "Thanks, Jenn. You probably saved my life."

The use of her name made Jenn sit up just a little in her chair and she felt her ears getting warmer and the hairs stand on end.

"So, how do you know my name?" she replied. "We've never met."

"Sure we did. Remember that day I stopped by the old man's house?"

"You mean Mr. Braun?"

"Whatever."

"How do you know him?"

"He was a customer of mine."

"What, uh…what's your business?"

She knew. Of course she knew. Mr. Braun didn't hide the fact that he liked a little *mota* now and again, probably a holdover from his military days. She had whiffed the grassy scent of weed mingling with incense once when she had brought Kylie over to play with Cherokee and had literally turned around and walked the quarter mile back home. Didn't even peer back to see if Mr. Braun came to the door. It wasn't that she disrespected him for his choices; heck, she had toked up back in high school, but she wanted to protect Kylie. Someday she'd try it, too, Jenn was sure, but until then…

"Man," the kid said, motioning his hand toward the wound, "it hurts. Hurts bad."

"We've got to get you to a doctor," Jenn said. "The problem is my phone has no service."

"Got a land line?"

Jenn frowned as she looked at him, as if to say, *Look around you.*

"Sorry, that was dumb. I can make it 'til the storm passes," he said.

"What's your name?" she replied.

The kid just smiled and winced again as he leaned back into the couch, obviously trying hard not to touch the bandanna, though it was taking all his will power not to do so. By now the wound was clotting, she surmised, and the surprise of being stabbed was wearing off, meaning the pain was probably getting worse. Was he going into shock? She couldn't remember the warning signs from her nursing classes. Best idea was to get his mind off of his pain with idle banter until she got cell service back.

"Ashton," he said.

"Well, nice to officially meet you, Ashton," Jenn said, repositioning her backside on the cold metal seat of the folding chair. "I don't suppose you want to tell me why you were out at Mr. Braun's homestead during the worst storm in years?

"Doing a deal," he replied with no hesitation. "That old man was a good customer of mine. Would buy in bulk, pay in cash, no questions asked. Dream customer as a matter of fact. Until tonight."

This kid is candid, I'll give him that, Jenn thought.

"So, how did you get stabbed?" she said. "Did Mr. Braun do it?"

"Yeah, that old bastard."

"Why?"

"He wouldn't pay."

"What happened?"

"I killed him and then set his house on fire."

Jenn sat up again as the words floated over the room like a stench from the apartment bathroom after Armando soiled the porcelain with Taco Bell. Candid, yeah.

"Wait, what?" she said. "You *killed* him?"

"Yeah." Ashton winced again. "I had to. You can't have customers who don't pay. Bad for business. Sends the wrong message to other customers. Makes them wonder what your toleration limits are."

The sky opened some more, if that was possible, and the pinpricks on the trailer's roof came together in one cacophony, an orchestra that was complemented by the drums of thunder echoing across the valley. It was a stupid idea, but for the briefest of moments, Jenn had considered running, just gathering up Kylie in her arms and dashing out the door, right past Ashton, whose head was tipped back and his eyes closed.

But he had upper-body muscle, even if one arm was out of commission. The hallway that led from one end of the trailer to the other seemed longer than it was, and she was just over five feet and 115 pounds dripping wet. No way she could hold him off and get to her car.

And he knew where she lived. He'd probably be gone by the time the cops showed up, and then one day soon he'd make his grand reentrance into her life.

No way. Not a chance. If she tried running, this wasn't going to end well.

Trapped.

***

The hell of it was that she fought off the creeping notion that she was attracted to him. A guy in great physical shape who's a little dangerous shows up at your doorstep, and you're single (well, a widow), a tad vulnerable and…what did she think was going to happen?

No. No. Armando was her true love.

"If I died, would you remarry?" she had asked him once as they lolled around in bed after sex.

"Nope," he said without hesitation. "Love you too much, babe. You changed my life."

That last part may have been true. She had met Armando at a saloon downtown; at the time, he had just finished his first tour in Afghanistan. He had eyes, sure, and a military build—better than Ashton's, she mused—but wow, did he have a potty mouth. Every other word out of his mouth started with the letter *F*, and that night, as the dark baritone of Johnny Cash jumped through the speakers, he even dropped the *C* word, in relation to the Taliban, while his eye roamed around the room.

That did it. She had gotten in his grille about what she thought was the most offensive word in the English language, hollering at him over "Ring of Fire," and he simply smiled and held up his arms as if to mea culpa. He bought her a drink and they talked until bar time, and then until dawn from his, eventually their, apartment around the corner.

Over time, the swearing dropped off significantly and that wandering eye? Gone. She found out later that he had been a guy slut, banging anything that appealed to him, and outside of one unfortunate drunken incident early in their relationship, that ceased as well. And then along came Kylie, which prompted them to get married, because that was what you did in Rapid City, South Dakota, when you got knocked up out of wedlock.

"Where is he?" Ashton's voice brought her back to reality, pointing to the wedding photo on the coffee table.

"Where is who?" Jenn replied after a split-second silence on which Ashton pounced.

"Husband or boyfriend?"

"Husband, and he'll be back soon," she said, trying to sound tough.

"Riiight. Guy like that looks like Army. I bet he's overseas or dead. Know how I know that?"

Kylie rolled over and whimpered in her sleep. Jenn didn't make a move.

"Flip-flops," he said. "I don't see any flip-flops around. See, military guys, like the ones at Ellsworth," the Air Force base on the other side of Rapid City, "they wear those big, heavy boots all day, and when they come home, the boots come off and the flip-flops go on. So either they're stashed in a closet or you got rid of them."

Armando used to live in flip-flops. He was even wearing them the night they met.

Silence.

"I'm sorry about your loss," Ashton said matter-of-factly before grimacing. "When did it happen?"

"I don't know what you're talking about," Jenn said. "You'd better leave."

Ashton chuckled, then seemed to catch himself, looking in the direction of Kylie, who whimpered again from somewhere nearby.

"Sorry, I don't want to wake your daughter," he said. "What's her name?"

"Like I said, you better leave."

But as if from Mother Nature herself, the wind whipped up in answer and slammed the side of the trailer, enough to push it ever so slightly. Waves of rain beat against the glass.

"Look, I'm not going to hurt you," he said, "or your little one. I'm a dealer, but I'm not a psycho. That old man down the way," he waved his arm in the direction of Mr. Braun's house, "that was business, nothing more, nothing less. You and I don't have business, and, in fact, I like you. You've got a little fire in you, plus you're cute. How old are you, twenty-five?"

"Too old for you," Jenn replied, now considering where Armando had kept his Glock. *That's right; it's in a locked box on the shelf of the closet right next to Kylie.* She strained to remember where the key was.

"Maybe, but we could still have some fun, you know?" Ashton said, looking around. "I've got some scratch. I could get you out of this dump, take you back to town, maybe even get a house. Take good care of you and your daughter."

Jenn's mind cut to a nice ranch with white siding and taupe trim and expertly manicured grass next to a driveway with her car and a red Schwinn with training wheels. And for a second, there she was waving to Ashton as he pulled up in his black late-1970s Camaro, wearing a Best Buy polo for some reason. The closing scene was him giving her a peck on the cheek and picking up Kylie and swinging her around before placing her down and saying, "What's for dinner, dear?"

No. Armando. Blackness, then his face and the cockeyed smile he had when he was up to something.

"You must think I'm a serial killer or something," he said. "Truth is I've never killed anybody before. Never had to. Customers always paid. This guy, Brown…"

"Braun."

"Whatever. I show up, he walks out with a gun," he says, shaping his fingers into a mock pistol, "and fires a couple in the air."

That part may have been true. Jenn had heard pops earlier that evening as the storm started to roll in. But she'd assumed it was thunder or some other atmospheric disturbance. It's South Dakota. Weather's weird here. No reason to think otherwise.

"I've gotta defend myself, right?" he said. "I had my gun, got out of the car, and it was like an Old West showdown. We pointed our guns at each other until we both agreed to set them down and discuss our differences like adults.

"Except that old bastard pulls out a Bowie knife and whips it at me," pointing at his arm. "He's standing over me, telling me I'm some little snot-nosed shit, no sense in my head, blah, blah, blah. I kicked him hard in the knee—cracked it, I think— knocked his ass down, and smoked him. Pulled him back into the house and lit that place up."

Jenn's right hand rose reflexively to her mouth.

"He was heavy," he went on, smiling.

"I don't want to…" she said, then catching herself and lowering her voice, "I don't want to know any more."

"Oh, come on, Jenn," he shot back. "You gotta admit I was justified."

"He was my friend!" Again, she had to work to lower her voice.

"He tried to kill me!" This time, he started on the high note and finished low, which she appreciated, for Kylie's sake.

Another trench of silence.

A red Schwinn. Kylie sailing through the air in Ashton's arms.

No. Armando.

Armando's gone.

Jenn turned to look at the digital clock in the kitchenette. That's right, no power. No red numbers to reassure her of normalcy. She squinted to try to force the building sleep out of her eyes. Silly, really. It was coming, like that storm outside, crossing the fields, tearing up anything in its path.

Ashton just stared at her. His hair was starting to dry, and his bangs lilted across his right eye, reminding her a little of her high school boyfriend, what was his name? Never mind.

"I go to school," he started again. "Western Dakota Tech. Studying business. Kind of ironic, isn't it? Business?" He chuckled again.

It was all Jenn could do to stop herself from saying, *Me too*, when he mentioned WDT. Could it be she had passed him on the main concourse or maybe Badlands Hall? No, he was probably in high school when she was there.

But she was convinced he would have caught her eye, and she had to shuttle that thought from her mind because of Armando. And maybe Kylie too.

"I don't want to work in retail, though," he went on, his hands animated. "Once again, kind of ironic. This whole drug thing, it's just a means to an end. Gotta pay for school somehow. If I want to get to the U. of South Dakota, need some scratch for tuition, books, the whole shootin' match."

Jenn leaned forward in her folding chair, less to make a point than relieve her tailbone ache. But it came off as a point.

"You seem like a smart kid," she said, wishing instantly she had said "smart guy" instead. Ashton frowned momentarily, then delivered his winning smile like a beacon across the dark room. Storm was moving off. Only intermittent flashes of lightning.

"You've obviously got a lot going for you…"

"Got an *A* in Econ last semester!" Big grin.

"See? So why put yourself in danger every time you leave your house? Don't you worry about…well, what happened tonight?" She motioned at his injury, and he looked down at it for a long while.

"I think it's the thrill," he finally said, frowning, thinking. "There's always been something about putting myself out there, getting that close to death, and then walking away. Like tonight. Your man knew that. That's why he went."

Jenn looked at the wedding photo. Armando stared back at her with his own soft caress of a smile, the kind that made her melt. The kind that, more often than not, led to the bedroom.

"No, he went back because he felt it was his responsibility," she said evenhandedly, though she wanted an edge to her voice. "He was against the Taliban and terrorists. He said they were cockroaches."

"Right, babe. It was the thrill of it all, trust me."

"No!" Louder than she intended. "No." *Better.* And *Babe*?

But all this exchange did was compel Jenn to consider the possibility that what Ashton was saying might be true. You face the biggest resistance in life during the process of admittance.

"Look," Ashton went on. "It probably wasn't about killing or some altruistic idea about saving the world. I would bet it was more about being out there with his boys, knowing that he might never have that chance again, in this life anyway. He probably didn't relish the possibility that he might not come home, but he was willing to take that chance."

"I just," she stammered, "I just don't buy that. We had a kid together and…"

"And what? A guy put himself ahead of his wife and daughter? Shocking."

"But…"

"Just a guess on my part," he said. "I don't know this dude from Adam. I just know the type. Deal with them all the time. You wouldn't believe how many customers I have over at Ellsworth." And then he stood, taking care to ensure the afghan was wrapped around his upper body. "Can I borrow this?" he said. "It's not my shade, but for a walk of shame, it'll have to do."

Jenn nodded and looked at the TV, but it was still off. She had been fingering her phone in her hand for the past half hour. Still no service. *Damn.*

"I enjoyed this little interlude," he said, "and I'd love to see you again sometime. Can we make that happen? And not on campus at Tech. Let's say, maybe Delmonico's?"

That was the first nice restaurant Armando had taken Jenn after they met.

She cut to a quaint table by the window, the candlelight creating sharp shades of shadow on Ashton's face, his deep voice in a low tone, though his eyes did most of the talking. Their meal finished, his arm—the one that was injured—snaked across the table in search of…something. Her hands were crossed in front of her, but now her right hand felt magnetized, as if it were drawn to his.

Their hands met, and she was struck by how soft and smooth they were in deep contrast his line of business. She'd expected roughhewn, calloused like a construction worker's, maybe, or how she imagined a longshoreman's hands might be.

"Come on," he said after a moment, then he stood. His jeans were tight and he wore a black blazer over a white T-shirt. Around his neck was a gold chain with Christ on His cross.

"Where are we going?" she said as she stood, realizing now she was wearing a red strapless dress and pumps—accoutrements she didn't own.

Ashton licked his thumb and touched her shoulder, then his own.

"Let's get out of these wet clothes," he said, sporting another winning grin.

Their lips met and she allowed her tongue to mate with his.

And then she was back on the couch, but he was still there, their lips entwined.

Armando stared back at her with a smile from the wedding photo on top of the coffee table.

***

The droning voice finally forced her awake at 5:24 a.m. "Let's get a look at Super Doppler 12. As you can see, the storm's moved eastward, and while we'll have some residue showers today, maybe a thunderstorm, weather should improve throughout the day," the gray-suited weatherman said. "Tonight, it's going to be dry and quiet, which I'm sure will be welcome to everyone in our viewing area."

She lifted her head with a start. Ashton had closed the inner door when he left. If there was anything to be grateful about, that was it. Couch was still damp, though.

Where was her phone?

On the floor. She picked it up. *Great! Service is back.* She dialed 911 and waited as it rang twice, then three times.

"Nine-one-one, what is your emergency?" came the woman's voice.

"My neighbor, my neighbor," she barked into the handset. "A guy killed my neighbor last night and came to my trailer after he did it. His name is Ashton, and he's tall, maybe 6-foot-2, brown hair…No, I didn't get a last name."

Knock-knock-knock.

Jenn frowned and threw her legs on the floor and took the three steps to the door and opened it.

"Hey, I saw the light on, and I wanted to see how you made out in the storm," Mr. Braun said with an unleashed Cherokee by his side.

People talk about jaws dropping in a situation like that, but it wasn't that way for Jenn. Hers tightened and her eyes widened. "But," she said, "but, I thought you were dead. A kid came here last night and told me…"

The old man ran his hand through his white hair and tugged on his ponytail. "Well, as you can see, that didn't happen. Right, Cherokee?" The dog stood up, wagged his tail, and though dogs don't smile, he appeared to do just that.

"I heard some popping last night that sounded like gunshots," Jenn said.

"Oh, some varmints out there got riled up by the storm. Coyotes probably. Cherokee here wanted to go after them, howled up a storm, but in the end, I took out Old Betsy and fired off a few shots. That learned 'em." Old Betsy was his .22 that hung on the wall of the old homestead.

"Then how do you explain this?" she said, pointing toward front of the door.

But there was no rug and, therefore, no blood.

He must have taken it. No evidence.

Somewhere in the distance, she could hear sirens.

"You all right?" Mr. Braun said, frowning. "You look like you had one hell of a night. Want to come over for a cup of joe? I bought donuts for the young'un."

Jenn was compelled to say exactly nothing. The sirens were getting closer.

"But I gotta wrap up by ten or so," he said. "My boy is coming over, Ashton is his name.

"You've seen him, I think, right? I should've introduced you. Guess he cut himself up good last night."

Your Shame is Overdue

Waubena, Minnesota

The sound of the chunky stamp slapping the inside cover of the book was the same to Jessica as it had been thirty-five years ago—an echo across the open space of the library's second floor that infiltrated the caverns of wall shelves and reverberated back to the desk in the corner next to the window.

Thoomp.

Cover closed. Next one opened. The same musty smell of thick tomes that hadn't been opened in years gave an aroma that was both putrid but alluring. What's inside, my dear?

Thoomp.

"Have you decided what to do?" Mrs. Berger asked. She bustled about while focused on a mountain of books on her desk, apparently to be decommissioned and donated.

The question. It's why Jessica had come back home to Waubena, Minnesota, after all that had happened. To answer it. Or rather to hear Mrs. Berger ask.

Because she couldn't ask herself. And if she did, the answer would be a lie.

Jessica did love her husband. Andy might be kind of dorky and set in his ways with some odd idiosyncrasies, but he was a good provider to her and their three children: Aiden (12), Claire (9), and Devin (6).

But that conference in Atlanta was…wow. The sales guy, the dinner, the drinks, his innuendo, and her wobbly courage to return it with a smile.

The trip upstairs to his hotel room. Him first, her five minutes later.

The act itself. Oh my God. The act.

The first thing Jessica thought of as he lay there snoring was not what Andy would do. If he found out. Holding it in, of course, was an option.

No, it was what Mrs. Berger would say.

Thoomp.

"I'm not surprised it happened," Mrs. Berger said, still not looking up from her pile of books. "You were always a comely young lady."

She'd used the same phrase back when Jessica was in high school and Mrs. Berger's hair still had streaks of brown in what was becoming a nest of smoky braids. She would shake her head when Jessica showed up for her English tutoring sessions in short shorts, tan legs, white moccasins, and perhaps a tank top or even a tube top if she was feeling particularly attractive that day.

Mrs. Berger on the other hand? She always seemed to be wearing the same beige sweater and brown skirt that traveled well below her knees, brown panty hose, and sensible orthopedic shoes. She looked like…well, a librarian.

"The fact that you haven't lost your looks doesn't excuse your actions, however," she went on, grabbing a new pile of books. "For that reason, I must counsel you to consider reporting this incident to your husband and with immediacy."

Thoomp.

"I knew you'd say that," Jessica replied as she turned toward the window and looked out. Still the same Waubena. Uncle Paul's Toy Store. The Bellyburner Burger Joynt. Wink's Photography. The Waubena-Wilson Bridge stood resolute over the turbid Mississippi in the gray distance as it always had. But there was the new as well, which suggested a burg in the throes of transition. Blazin' Tattoos. Hookah Lounge. A White Castle under construction.

Jessica turned around and Mrs. Berger's seat was empty.

"If I told Andy," Jessica said, "*if* I had the courage, that is, he'd be devastated. It would fucking destroy him."

"Language, please," came Mrs. Berger's faint voice from somewhere among the stacks. "Remember your Shakespeare."

Thou art a boil, a plague sore.

King Lear, Act II, Scene ii.

Jessica recalled Mrs. Berger's counsel after Jimmy Della Ponte broke up with her in the ninth grade. Jessica had stormed into the library, cursing with guns ablaze, and Mrs. Berger just listened, then dropped the *King Lear* line, followed by: "It is not worth using salty, vulgar language, even if one is a cad. There are alternatives to swearing." And that's when they began studying *King Lear*, which to this day is Jessica's favorite Shakespearean tragedy.

Andy was no cad. He was the sweetest person Jessica had ever met, which made her infidelity that much more…astounding? Perhaps that's not the right word. Too dramatic. Maybe surprising was better.

Andy was the kind of person who still opened doors for her, waited to eat until she sat down, and sent flowers just to say, *I love you.*

He was deeply involved in his children's activities: Aiden's wrestling, Devin's theater, and Claire's gymnastics, although he was never totally comfortable standing around with the other dance moms while their daughters cavorted and cartwheeled.

He was a good man.

Mrs. Berger was still skulking somewhere in the stacks when Jessica, turning from the window to Mrs. Berger's desk, said, "If I tell him, don't you think that would immediately end our marriage?" She didn't know how that big stack of books had disappeared because she hadn't heard a cart roll up or roll away. There was a sepia photo of an unsmiling

Mrs. Berger in front of the Eiffel Tower, circa post-World War II; a color image from the '80s of her niece Evelyn in a purple jumper; and a tiny Buddha she had acquired on a trip to Thailand the summer after the Jimmy Della Ponte incident.

"Not necessarily," came Mrs. Berger's voice from somewhere still far away. "Though I have seen your husband from afar, and he appears to be levelheaded and dependable. I speculate he will indeed be, shall we say, 'troubled' by your choice, and after a period of inevitable sadness, and perhaps furious behavior, however, I believe there would be reconciliation. Provided you are not in love with this other man."

His name was Jack (she didn't get a last name), and he was from another division in the company. He was good-looking, sure—even with a slight paunch—and very good in bed, as it turned out. But he was as arrogant as sin, the kind of man who referred to liberals as "Libtards," which Jessica thought insensitive because her Devin had Down syndrome. Jack couldn't have known that, but in retrospect, she was sure it wouldn't have mattered.

Jack was in sales, so he was a smooth and convincing raconteur. Nobody would find out, he told her afterward, as long as she didn't say anything. He certainly wouldn't. Spoken like a man who had been there.

Why did she do it? Oh my God, why?

"Because there was something missing in your life," Mrs. Berger said in answer to her unspoken question. She suddenly back at her desk, though no footsteps had announced her arrival. A new stack of books was piled high to her left, and she began stamping again. "There was a deficit. You needed to fill the deficit. Once again," she said while not looking at Jessica, "I don't approve of what you did, but I can perhaps understand why the action was taken."

It was true that date nights, long walks, and sex had headed to the wayside of the highway of their marriage once the kiddos had come 'round. It was almost an effort to work in any one of those things in between demanding jobs, committees, practices, and everything else that made up an average day. Probably not that much different than any other couple in modern Middle America.

But Jessica had acted out and created a vagary of titanic proportion.

Thoomp.

"You strike me as defeated," Mrs. Berger said. "But I implore you to recall the words of Dostoyevsky, 'To live without hope is to cease to live.'"

"From *The Brothers Karamazov*," Jessica said, this time not looking at Mrs. Berger, but perceiving someone at the end of the stacks near the stairs. *Familiar*. This time she heard the steps coming in her direction.

"Correct," Mrs. Berger replied. "I am heartened by the fact that you remember the things I taught you, because it means you placed importance on it."

"Well, you were an island of reality the middle of the junkyard of my youth," Jessica replied and cracked a smile, recalling all of those days when she wanted to give up because of her disgruntlement with schoolwork; her parents grievances; or boys, boys, boys. There was always a book with a line that seemed a salve for those things that were ailing her.

That was true even now.

"When you face up to the truth, that truth will set you free," Mrs. Berger said, adjusting her backside on her wooden, slatted chair that had never struck Jessica as very comfortable.

"That's from the Good Book, my young friend," she went on.

"Yes, I know. John 8:32."

"Then you must allow the truth to set you free of this cage in which you have placed yourself."

"But…"

"There is no 'but'; there is right, and there is wrong."

"Life is not usually so black and white."

Now Mrs. Berger turned to Jessica and their eyes met for the first time that afternoon. "Is it? Your actions were wrong, but keeping those actions from the one who can set you free is a travesty."

Jessica turned, walked toward the window again, and placed her hands on the ancient radiator. It was summer in Waubena, the metal was cold, and her fingers found their way along the slats she remembered from her youth, even before Mrs. Berger. Outside, two teenage girls bounced up the street. One wore tight jean shorts and could have been Jessica decades ago.

Thoomp.

She turned on her heel, the wooden floorboards creaking, and peered at the desk, which was empty again. Completely clean and dusted with a placard that read, *In Honor of Mrs. Eloise Berger, Librarian, 1921-1984.*

And under that were the words of Anton Chekhov: "Knowledge is of no value unless you put it into practice."

Creaky steps now stopped. "Hey, babe?" came a voice, and Jessica looked up. "Who were you talking to?"

Andy.

She considered her response for a moment and replied, "A ghost." Then she said, "There's something I need to talk to you about."

KNOWN BUT TO GOD

Arlington, Virginia

Couldn't have missed the sign. Shaped like a large dinner platter, it may as well have been another armed guard. Plenty of them stalking around on this most solemn day.

Silence and Respect, it commanded, and it stood at the point where the president would enter the proceedings.

To his right the steps that constituted the viewing area at the Memorial Amphitheater were mostly full of straight-lipped, nattily dressed citizens, except for a few teenagers in the front row in loud sweatshirts and baggy, frayed jeans, elbowing each other and snickering. No one said a word to them.

Margaret Smith stood to their left, shaking her head. Time was, kids wore suits and dresses to this dignified occasion and stood like statues as the president laid the annual wreath at the Tomb of the Unknown Soldier. But times had changed. In fact, for Margaret Smith, it felt as if time had passed her by, which was perhaps the biggest irony of all.

Like Christmas or Easter was to other families, Armistice Day was *her* event, the culmination of a year of fervent planning and waiting and wonderment.

Maybe this was the year. That was always the hope, at least.

The president took calculated steps across carefully carved concrete rectangles; an Army general at his side matched his movements. As they neared the marble tomb monument, a white-gloved bugler breathed into his instrument for the first time. The president placed his right hand over his heart, and the general saluted.

Margaret Smith ducked her head under the stanchion and briskly strode toward them, the frills of her white nurse's dress trailing behind her lazily in the crisp November breeze. Just then, the breeze picked up from the easterly direction of the city and stung her face, causing her eyes to water. The president seemed to flinch too.

No one moved or spoke. The dark-suited, sunglassed Secret Service agents stood still and warily glanced from left to right.

Same as every year. They didn't see her or hear the click of her sensible heels as she strode with purpose and crossed herself for luck as she arrived next to the pair.

"Mr. President," she began softly, as she did every year, standing on her tiptoes and craning her neck so she was face to face with the man. "Mr. President, can you hear me?"

His handsome face and prominent jaw, which she had known since he was a star football player at the University of Michigan and then for the Chicago Bears and finally as Speaker of the House of

Representatives, remained completely still. Almost a year into his first term, his wavy chestnut hair had more than a few flecks of gray, residue from the stressors of the job he was elected to in a landslide. Partisan politics had nothing on football.

"Mr. President, if you can hear me, please tell these people, these fellow Americans, that a soldier isn't buried here," Margaret Smith said in a raised voice. She nearly added, *It's me*, but then caught herself, as if that information was somehow a secret, something spoken of in hushed tones outside the Pentagon. Like no one should know, because there was no saving face.

Nope, couldn't hear her. Same as every year from President Harding on. The closest she had come to being liberated from her predicament was during the administration of John Fitzgerald Kennedy, when she had screamed in tears at the young, handsome president during his Armistice Day address. By that time had become Veterans Day, but she preferred Armistice Day. He had actually turned toward her and made eye contact, stopping mid-word and frowning slightly. But then he smiled his perfect smile, picked up his train of thought, and that was that.

It was 1963. It was the year she had been standing next to a (suited) youngster who blurted out, "There he is!" when President Kennedy arrived on foot with other elected officials and the color guard at the tomb monument. Everyone snickered, including Margaret Smith.

Of course, that was JFK's last Armistice Day. Any hope she had at getting through to him in '64 died that terrible day in Dallas. LBJ and Nixon after him were stone-faced, soulless suits.

Margaret Smith turned away from the current president and took a few steps toward the cubist tomb monument, being careful not to step on the Unknown Soldier of World War II's grave.

Carved into the west side of the monument were the words, *Here Rests in Honored Glory an American Soldier Known but to God.*

She had chafed at that language since she had stood by and watched it being erected in the early 1930s. True, she had been a member of the U.S. Army Nurse Corps and saw her fair share of death and broken men who prayed for death, but she was no soldier.

She had loved one though.

It's why she was here.

Love.

Love and the mere possibility of loss can often trigger the irrational.

That's why she had insisted on climbing aboard the Ford ambulance that day in 1918 as it trundled from outside Lucy-le-Bocage toward the oat fields west of Belleau Wood, not even a mile away. The young Negro private who was driving—Moses was his name—tried to protest, but she would have none of it. Frank was up there, in the middle of the wood, deep in the midst of some of the worst fighting of that great and terrible war. The worried faces of the runners carrying communiqués past the field hospital indicated that things were not going well: casualties were mounting, and retreat wasn't out of the question.

Like Margaret Smith, Frank was a doughboy from the Midwest, a place called Oconomowoc, Wisconsin. When President Wilson had declared war on the dirty Germans, he had signed up, preferring not to wait for the draft. At the same time, hundreds of miles away in sleepy Waterloo, Iowa, she had volunteered for the Army Nurse Corps.

They'd met on the first afternoon of the battle. Frank was leaning against a pile of crates outside the field hospital west of Lucy-le-Bocage, his right arm in a bloody makeshift sling thanks to a Hun sharpshooter whose aim was just a hair off.

He was thick and muscular with a warm, kind smile under a thatch of black hair. He also possessed an almost elegant way of speaking, pronouncing his words carefully, much unlike the cheeky, fast-talking boys from places like Chicago and New York, who were only after what was underneath a nurse's britches. Another nurse, Fanny someone from Indiana, had gotten (shhh!) pregnant!

"I guess I had a bit of an accident," was the first thing Frank had ever said to her as he broke into a crooked smile, which was as attractive to her as his pearly eyes, even in that godforsaken place with the sound of heavy guns booming in the distance. "Can you patch me up?"

She did and the doctors sent him to Meaux for a weeklong convalescence in a makeshift hospital that occupied a bombed-out church. When Margaret Smith wasn't working in the field hospital, she was in Meaux. There, she and Frank simply talked: him about working in his family's tailor shop on Wisconsin Avenue in downtown Oconomowoc—her about Mama, her eight siblings, and the big red barn Daddy had erected to replace the one that had burnt down right before she departed for Europe. The conversations continued in her mind even when she was back on duty, comforting the shot-up, blown-up men who would never see the shores of home again.

But Frank had to return to the front, and the peculiar thing was that he'd wanted to; he'd felt it was his duty to his unit, his country, and his God to drive out the Huns from the wood and, ultimately, France itself. He was willing to put himself in harm's way for a greater good. The ambulance, with that same Negro private driving, idled with a *potato-potato-potato* sound from its engine. She looked deeply into Frank's eyes, losing herself in the pools of green and his childish dimples constructed of the remnants of his baby fat.

"You know, we should get..." he had said.

"Yes, oh yes," was her only response. She had kissed a few boys in her life, but for the first time, she had kissed a man, and it was as slow and fathomless as she had imagined it would be when pondering those things back on the farm.

But the fighting. Oh, the fighting. What was left of young, virile men like Frank continued to arrive as the battle pitched eviscerated souls that were often beyond help. One doughboy, who looked to be about sixteen, had lost both legs and was screaming for his mother. Then he suddenly stopped mid-sentence as he expired, his eyes and mouth still wide and open under his saucepan helmet.

She had had to look twice, because for a moment, she saw Frank.

Margaret Smith began seeing Frank in her mind a lot over the coming days, which was why she was in the passenger seat of that ambulance as it headed up the road toward the wood that afternoon.

"You crazy for goin' up there, ma'am," Private Moses said, concentrating on the dusty, pockmarked road. Great booms of shellfire came closer, followed by the subtle popping that took her a moment to realize was machine-gun fire, probably German. "The devil himself up there, takin' men by the truckload."

She ignored him. If the world was coming to an end, then Frank was all that mattered. If he was called by the Good Lord to die for Him, his country, and her, then she wanted to die with him.

It was crazy. How in God's precious Name was she going to find him in the muck and mud of the battlefield? The trees of the wood mere stalks due to the artillery from both sides. The wind picked up and blew thick, ebony smoke that made her flinch at the acrid smell and taste. Moses didn't say a word, just shook his head a few times at the veiled white lady next to him with a pensive look on her face.

They arrived at the 5th Marine HQ; dead doughboys on stretchers lined the side of the road, while others, still alive, awaited transport by Moses back to Lucy-le-Bocage area and relative safety. One soldier, leaning on his right elbow, whistled as the truck sauntered by. She didn't look in his direction, but if she had, she would have noticed his left arm was severed below the elbow.

Moses hadn't even stopped the truck in front of the tent before Margaret Smith jumped out and began running across the road toward the lush carpet of oats that was the precursor to the forbidding wood on its far side and the sounds of men fighting and dying.

"Hey!" came a voice. "What the hell are you doing?"

Another private, wielding a rifle with a long thin bayonet, ran toward her. She picked up the pace and dashed over a small berm, taking care not to trip on her skirt. The sound of gunfire was getting closer, and a pair of stretcher bearers were falling back with a blonde youngster—couldn't have been more than seventeen—with thick blood pouring out of a head wound.

He's not going to make it, she thought from experience as the stretcher bearers gave her a passing glance; the private was in close pursuit.

Suddenly, a gunshot from behind her, the bullet whizzing well past her right ear, finally got her attention.

"Stop!" the private said, and she did as he ran up. "Where do think you're going?"

Margaret Smith was out of breath and could only manage four words: "Got to find him."

"Who?"

Just then, a pair of battle-worn soldiers, one with a bandage wrapped around his dark curls, emerged from the wood. They were supporting a helmetless soldier who had been shot in the gut, the blood a great wine-colored sphere began under his uniform breast pocket and stopped above his belt. He wasn't walking, his legs dragged behind him.

Frank. Oh my God.

She caught herself momentarily—was that blasphemy? She couldn't remember.

Lord, please, please…no.

Frank's head was limp, chin resting on the collar of his uniform blouse, and she could hear absolutely nothing as she dashed toward him. Not even the private wailing behind her in protest like an overloaded mule on the farm back home.

Not even the sound of a German artillery piece about a mile away unleashing a barrage in the direction of the American base of operations on the other side of the wood.

Each step seemed to take an eternity as she ran across the oat field, nearly falling once. Her shouts of "Frank! Frank!" were somehow shrouded as if a veil of distortion had been affixed to her words.

But he looked up. He looked up! And he smiled. Years later, JFK's soft, tender smile reminded Margaret Smith of that day on the battlefield.

The explosion came directly overhead, and Margaret Smith was terrorized for a split second by a pain so great and terrible that there was no doubt the end was nigh.

Then it was eerily quiet, like the veil had been lifted. She stood at the foot of a crater and stared down at what was left of her mortal body; somehow, she knew it had been hers. Somehow. Bones, mostly, her white nurses' uniform was burning into nothingness as the smoke drifted toward Moses and his truck, which had been knocked over by the blast.

"Margaret," came a sweet male voice from the opposite side of the crater.

Frank still had that same smile on his face, but his uniform was clean and appeared expertly laundered, puttees wrapped tightly above his boots. She held out her arms and looked down, realizing the pleats of her angelic-white skirt were straight and true.

Had they…survived?

Yes, but…how? What was happening?

"It's perfect here," Frank said. "Just perfect."

Margaret Smith frowned as Frank held out his hand toward her. An intense white light cracked through what looked like a door opening behind him.

"I'll be waiting right here for you," Frank went on, pointing downward. "Behold, you are beautiful, my beloved, truly delightful." Song of Solomon 1:16.

He was someplace else. He wasn't at Belleau Wood anymore.

He was with the Good Lord Himself.

She took a running step toward him, but the door closed, and he was gone. She fell into the crater and banged her knee against a smoldering piece of metal, presumably from the shell, and landing right next to the open eye pits of a skull.

Her human skull.

She had never screamed so loud and so long, not even when she was bitten by the corn snake in the barn back home as a toddler.

Next, Margaret Smith found herself standing in a dusty alcove of the Châlons city hall in France. Dark-stained wooden planks led to four caskets in the rotunda; hers was the third from the left.

She had followed her bones from the battlefield to the Aisne-Marne cemetery near the foot of Hill 142, a hotly contested piece of real estate the U.S. Marines had finally secured after nearly a month of fighting, most of which she'd witnessed in person. Her grave marker simply said *Unknown*. She sat cross-legged in front of it on the warmest days of summer, rainy fall deluges, and the winter snows of 1919 and 1920.

One day, though, in May 1921—Memorial Day in the U.S., as it turned out—what was left of her bones were dug up, casketed, and brought to Châlons-sur-Marne to join three others.

The ceremony was short and somber. An American soldier she didn't recognize, a Sergeant Younger, placed a handful of white roses on her casket and addressed the crowd of local dignitaries, residents, and lots and lots of soldiers from armed privates to French, American, and even British generals.

"No one knows who this soldier was, but he has a family back home, and perhaps the honor on which he is bestowed today will ease the pain caused by this awful conflict," Sergeant Younger read from a crumpled piece of paper while leaning on his cane. Apparently, he had been wounded in combat. Like Frank.

Margaret Smith said nothing. She turned on her heel and found herself on the street outside, droplets of rain beginning to fall.

Later that year, in the new Memorial Amphitheater in Arlington National Cemetery, President Warren Harding, who was not quite a year into his term, made his own address on Armistice Day. Her casket was snugly buried under the white-marble sarcophagus.

"The name of the man whose body lies before us took flight with his imperishable soul," the president had said, his white hair matching his starched collar. "We know not whence he came, but only that his death marks him with the everlasting glory of an American dying for his country."

Always he. Him. Couldn't possibly be her or she.

She ran from the ceremony's rear to the podium, her white heels clicking on the concrete, to where the chubby-faced, bow-tied president was pontificating.

"Mr. President, I am *not* a soldier!" she screamed, but Harding went on as if she weren't there.

Margaret Smith was all alone in the world.

She found a place to live in the city, an old brownstone near Pennsylvania Avenue, which afforded her brisk daily walks to the White House and Capitol Hill. Arlington and the Tomb of the Unknown Soldier was a short train ride across the Potomac, though if she wanted to, she could just think about it and she would be there. But the train was more entertaining and allowed her at least some sense of normalcy.

So it went for more than nine decades. Presidents came and went. Wars started and ended in Europe and the Pacific and in places she had never heard of, like Korea, Vietnam, Iraq, and Afghanistan. Over time, three more graves had been added to the west of the tomb monument. One of them, from the Vietnam War, was actually identified in 1998 through some fancy scientific process called DNA testing. They belonged to a man, a jet pilot, she understood, based on the news reports she could read over shoulders on the Metrorail Blue Line.

Why couldn't the same testing be done for her remains? Surely it would confirm that a woman's remains were in the tomb monument, and maybe, just maybe, they would be able to use the results to find her descendants. Then the world would know who Margaret Smith, U.S. Army Nurse Corps, was.

Instead, she was relegated to hoping upon hope every Armistice Day that this was the year. She would scream to get the attention of the current president and then head home in disappointment.

For more than 100 years. Astonishing.

If only God would reopen that door. She was convinced her Frank would still be waiting for her there.

If only God would have mercy on her soul.

During the actor Ronald Reagan's first term as president, she'd even considered the possibility, albeit briefly, that perhaps God didn't exist. A god that would punish a faithful servant sounded like an angry despot and, therefore, not a deity worth serving.

But she quickly shooed that thought from her mind as blasphemy. God was God, light was light, and she was imperfect, no matter how many times she went to church. That was one thing that didn't change: every Sunday she could be found at Washington National Cathedral, raising her voice to the Lord, even getting in line for communion, though she always felt a little silly in her Ragtime Era nurses' uniform.

There must be some reason she wasn't able to make it through that door. But what was it? For Margaret Smith, it was the literal and rhetorical question for the ages.

So on that Armistice Day morning, as she prepared herself in the predawn darkness for her trip on the Blue Line to Arlington National Cemetery. Her veil was just as clean and true as it had been that day in the crater when the door opened and then closed with her love behind it. She fingered the red cross in the center for a moment and placed it upon her head, tucked her sandy hair under it, and then affixed it with bobby pins. She slipped into her nurse's uniform, also pristine, and then stepped into her sensible flats. She chuckled to herself at the terms people used nowadays; there was never anything "sensible" about women's shoes, not even in her era. Or any era, she wagered.

She endured a Blue Line ride sitting near a young white punk listening to something called "rap" music, the rhythm and syncopation so deep and pungent that the only thing worse was the language the singer used to convey his views about society. How unfair there was no opportunity. How one had to "get theirs" or die trying. How it was acceptable to shoot those who displeased you.

It got to the point where Margaret Smith was compelled to close her eyes, imagine the tomb monument, and then in a quiet whisper she was there, behind the stanchion, watching the president and the Army general attendant enter the proceedings. As per usual, she approached the president and, once again unsuccessful in getting his attention, she awaited his address at the podium.

What was interesting about that morning was the fact that the First Lady wasn't present. The obnoxious news had been speculating for months of a rift between the president and his comely, redheaded wife; was it possible they would divorce? Margaret Smith found this highly improbable, considering the apparent indiscretions of Franklin Roosevelt, John Kennedy, and other presidents along the way. But in the new wave of communications one could access via their telephone, including a phenomenon called social media, talk was rife that divorce was indeed a possibility, that the president was desperate to save his marriage yet still manage the affairs of the country.

Marriages in this new century were strained by the weight of expectations, which were often impossible to meet. Perhaps that characterized this president's marriage.

She stood by herself in front of the podium, hands clasped at her waist. The two Secret Service agents behind the president paid her no mind. The speech began as she expected: the same canned verbiage about the "soldiers only God knows" who had made the supreme sacrifice for a grateful nation that enjoys the privileges today those men had fought and died for.

But what about me? Margaret Smith wondered. A seed suddenly began to sprout within the depths of her being, growing up into her throat and exploding into the afternoon sun.

"What about me? What about all the women who have fought and died for our country?" She began in a stiff voice that was curt yet respectful of the executive office, but eventually evolved into a ghastly demonstration atypical of a proper woman from 1918. She had even used colorful language forbidden by her mother. "Use your words of frustration to glorify your Lord," mother had said one morning after church when she had used the words "damn fool" to describe her younger, irascible brother.

But facing another year of denial, another year of hoping, another year of angst, she questioned why, like Jesus, God had forsaken her. And it spilled like beans on the counter.

"I. Am. Unknown!" she shrieked, in the midst of still faces, even those disruptive teenagers. The president prattled on, making eye contact with audience members on either side.

"...my wife had pointed out..."

"Lord, have mercy on me!"

"...that there have been..."

Margaret Smith grabbed her veil and threw it at the president; it passed through his body as if he hadn't been standing there.

He stopped briefly and looked across the expanse of people to the tomb monument and beyond to Washington, D.C., and the vastness of America.

A pause, she guessed, for effect.

Then he began again: "My lovely wife, the woman who brings stability to my life and that of our children and a veteran of the Gulf War, reminded me of the thousands of women who have served in our Armed Forces since revolutionary times, including those who were missing in action.

"They, those missing women, are truly known but to God for their heroism," he said. "It is an embarrassment that they have been forgotten by history, but they deserve our respect just as much as the millions who lost their lives defending our great republic."

He then stopped and stared at Margaret Smith.

Was that a wink?

"Be released from the bonds of our lack of foresight," he went on. "Be released into the arms of God. As for me and my fellow Americans, you are not forgotten."

He nodded at her as if to encourage her to turn and she did. Frank, still in his perfectly pressed uniform, stood beside a rectangle of breathtaking light. He held out his hand in the same motion as he had at the crater so long ago.

"Where've ya been?" he said with a wry grin. "I've missed ya."

Dinner and a Movie

Tampa, Florida

He lifted his right hand high in the air and sprinkled cilantro onto the sole filets in the Pyrex baking dish like verdant raindrops. That was his secret: fresh cilantro, because it added a layer of flavor to an otherwise mild fish, which is why I had to find some. Thank goodness for Trader Joe's.

I was lounging at the dining room table and halfway through a Diet Coke, wishing I could have been sipping a nice, light pinot grigio because that goes best with white fish. But I had been clean at that point for almost eighteen months, and while I was oh so tempted, I had to stay that way. I knew my limitations. One led to two; two led to ten.

"You see, Atropos is one of the Three Fates," Peter said, opening the creaky oven door, which probably hadn't been privy to such a succulent meal in its long lifetime. Mediterranean baked sole with a buttery lime sauce, capers, and, like I said, fresh cilantro. Yummo.

"Her sisters are Klotho and Lachesis, and they work together to fashion a person's life from beginning to end," he said, wiping his hands on a dingy yellow kitchen towel. "I work for Atropos, who ends people's lives by cutting the thread of life that was spun by Klotho and measured out by Lachesis. Does that make any sense?"

"So you're here to kill me?" I replied.

He stopped wiping his hands and looked at me with a thoughtful gaze, his eyes rolling toward the ceiling.

"'Kill' is such a harsh word," he said, returning his eyes to mine. "Think of it as a logical transition, and you know what? The good news is that since you've straightened yourself out, you've pleased Zeus and the gods, so your eternal destination is one you're gonna enjoy. Now, if I would have come to call, say, three years ago, it might have been a different story."

I sat up in my chair and burst out laughing. I had no idea a history professor could be that funny. *Cutting the thread.* If I had still been in Hollywood, with all their religious wackos and gurus and faith healers running around, I might have bought what he was selling.

His name was Peter Stone, and he was a professor at the University of South Florida specializing in, among other things, the ancient Greeks and mythology. He had arrived in my life last week after his six-month research sabbatical in Athens. I was at a Starbucks, nursing a decaf grande, when he sat down at my spartan (see what I did there?) two-person table.

"Hey, aren't you Kimber Kaplan?" he'd said with a gleam in his eye. "I was a big fan of *The Little One* back in the day."

A bit about me. Yes, I am Kimber Kaplan. Yes, I starred in a TV show called *The Little One* for five seasons in the mid-eighties, which was cancelled when I hit puberty. Like many child actors, I became typecast in that role, and Hollywood can be a hellish existence if you're typecast: the rejections by producers who think you're "not quite right" for a part; the "Where are they now?" paparazzi shooting montages for the *National Enquirer*; the autograph requests from weirdos who want to say they bedded my character. Less-than-timely return phone calls from your agent who tells you to be realistic about your future in showbiz.

And on top of all that, finding out that the people you thought were your friends really never were.

"Yeah, I'm Kimber," was my curt reply, tucking my lower lip under my upper teeth.

He introduced himself, and I was relieved he didn't ask for an autograph or, worse, a selfie. It was cool that day, at least for Tampa, and he was wearing a light-blue dress shirt without a tie, a tweed blazer, and jeans. I figured either writer or academic. Turned out he was both.

We talked for awhile about how I'd split my youth between Tampa and Hollywood, my one and only semester at USF, what I was doing now (not much), and a little about his work.

He was intriguing. I could talk to him. And it helped that he had dashing gray temples and a hint of an accent, maybe Boston or somewhere else in New England. I'd learned a lot about accents during my short-lived acting career, and I'm pretty good at picking them out. Like Wisconsin and Minnesota people really trill their *O*s. Canadians are worse.

It was a Tuesday morning when we met, and we exchanged email addresses. I was doubtful it would go anywhere, but sure enough, by lunchtime Thursday, he emailed to ask if he could cook me dinner. Apparently, he had a great recipe for sole that he got from a colleague. Was I up for that?

A guy had never cooked for me. Ever. We always went out on Tuesday nights in Hollywood.

"Just to prove I'm not a psychopath, here's a link to my CV," he wrote, and I clicked on the link. Seemed legit, author of the apparently critically acclaimed *The Question of the Gods*, which I surmised had to do with Zeus, Hermes, Athena, all the usual suspects. I had learned about them from my private tutor in my trailer between shoots.

He came over to my upstairs apartment in Historic Kenwood—I did manage to save a few bucks from my short acting career—and brought everything he needed to cook, including utensils and the Pyrex baking dish. I don't cook. The only thing I'm good at making is reservations.

We talked for awhile about this and that and somehow landed on the topic of his current project, another book. He said it would break new ground in our understanding of the perceptions of birth, life, and death in antiquity. *Our understanding*. As if I were part of the "our." I think he meant his colleagues and students.

I guess it was interesting, for as much as I understood, and he concluded by grabbing the big knife that he used to cut the sole, pointing it at me, and stating in an imperious voice, "I'm Atropos' servant."

"Who's Atropos?" said I, and you know what happened after that. I laughed.

But he had a look that made me wonder if he really was a psychopath. Or psychotic. I can't remember the difference, and I'm not near a computer to look up the definitions on Dictionary.com.

"You're going to stab me?" I said, feigning fear, though a pinch of it had wormed into the back of my brain.

He lowered the knife and said, "No, it doesn't work that way. I personally can't use violence. I'm not allowed to stick you with this. The only thing I can do in that realm is stop a heart from beating, which doctors call natural causes. But I *can* influence people to do things—say a drug overdose or make a wrong turn into the wrong neighborhood. Things like that."

Okay, get a grip, Kaplan. This guy is psycho.

But he went on, and I played along. "Every person's life comes to its logical end, which is determined by Atropos and her sisters before you're even a twinkle in your folks' eyes," he said. "I'm merely a means to that end. I guess you'd say literally."

"So basically, you're the angel of death?"

"I *hate* that phrase," he said, gritting his teeth and shaking his head. "It always seemed so, I don't know, crass. Like what I do is so evil or something."

"But isn't it? You're killing people. Or at least responsible for their deaths."

"Like I said, everyone's existence is finite. All existence has to come to end at some point. I'm just a tool."

I snickered because it just sounded funny. *A tool.*

But I still wasn't buying it. *Would you?*

"Okay, so how long have you been doing this?" I asked.

"Time eternal, babe. Time eternal."

"Jesus."

"He's a great example of what I do. Like the Stones said, I ensured Pontius Pilate washed his hands and sealed His fate. In fact," and he seemed pleased with himself, "*I* planted that idea in Mick Jagger's brain. Just for fun. Kind of like a joke."

"That tune says he's Lucifer," I replied. "You're the devil?"

"Don't think one dimensionally." He said the words with equal emphasis: Don't. Think. One. Dimensionally. "Golly, you humans only perceive things in linear terms—right and wrong, liberal and conservative, good and evil. Please. Not everything has an opposite."

"Doesn't it? I mean, you're talking life and then death and…"

He cut me off and placed his right index finger to his mouth, as if telling a kid to shut up. "Look, we're not having this conversation," he said. "You're distracting me, and I've got work to do."

And with that, my heart started beating faster. I'd never had heart palpitations, not even when I met George Clooney (again…see what I did there?), but it was like an engine revving. After a few seconds I couldn't even count the beats, and I fell off the chair onto all fours.

I was so close to the floor that I could see tiny flecks of grit in the lines between the hardwood floor boards. I was probably three feet away from the oven, and down there, the sole was just starting to smell good. I remember thinking that he was right, the cilantro did make a difference. His spit-shined penny loafers took a few steps toward me.

"What if I told you that the gods of antiquity, the gods of Greece, weren't a myth?" his words floated down to me from high above. "What if I told you they were real and had been banished into the pages of history books by the Judeo-Christian tradition and later by Islam? Yet, their work continues. Everything is orchestrated by the gods, even your birth, life, and imminent death."

I was sweating by now and the start of a migraine. For whatever reason, I managed to shout, "But I'm Kimber Kaplan!"

"Yes, yes you are," he said, and I could tell he bent down because I felt a hand on the back of my head. "But remember, fame and fortune don't impress Zeus and the rest of Mount Olympus. Achilles found that out the hard way. Of course, *The Iliad* was just a story by Homer, but believe you me, there have been many renowned people throughout history who met me at a young age and thought their fame would save them."

I was drifting in and out of consciousness as he listed them off, but the only ones I can remember were Alexander the Great, Nero, James Dean, and Tupac. However, there were a lot more. A whole lot more.

"Do you enjoy it?" I gasped as my face hit the floor and a shard of pain exploded through my nose like the palm-heel strike I learned about in self-defense class, coincidentally in my only semester at USF.

Then my heartbeat started to slow. Down, down, down until it was just about back to normal. I lifted my face off the floor, and I could see the imprint of my sweaty nose and cheek on the hardwood. A little blood, too, though my nose wasn't gushing. Just a few drips.

"That's an interesting question," he said, still standing over me. I pictured a frown and his arms folded as if he were giving a lecture and a student asked a question he didn't think was academic. I couldn't lift my head to see him, though.

"Do I enjoy what I do?" he repeated. "Hmmm. You know, most people never meet me in person, like you are. When they do, they usually beg for their life, or ask why, oh, why are you taking me from my family and friends? Sam Kinison did that, by the way. What prompted that question?"

Truthfully, it was what had popped into my oxygen-starved brain at that time. But I took a few deep breaths. "Just answer me."

Silence for a few seconds, and then: "The truth is that I've never thought about it. It's just my job. No more, no less. I go where I'm directed and do what I have to."

I rolled on my back and stared up at Professor Peter Stone. "But," I said, the sweat sticking my black tank top to the floor, "if you're doing this to thousands of people every day, maybe millions, do you get off on other people's misery? Is that it?"

The sole was really starting to smell good by now, and my stomach made a slight rumble.

"If you're gonna do this to me now, I want to know," I said. "I want to know if you're going to enjoy putting me down."

"It's odd, the only other person to ask me something like this, if you can believe it, was Napoleon," he said. "He asked me if what I do is honorable, like a soldier. The question caught me off guard, but the more I thought about it, the more I didn't care for the implication. I had administered his cancer years before upon Atropos' command, and the end had finally come. And now he's asking me if I felt I did my job in the spirit of nobility. I almost let him live just to watch his suffering increase, but that would have been wrong. Even I'm not a sadist. Humans are. I merely come to collect."

Silence again, broken by the digital timer on the fridge that my mom had given me for Christmas, along with the set of kitchen towels and a number of other domestic sundries. He touched a button and the *beep-beep-beep* ceased before placing his thumb and his forefinger at the cusp of his chin, like he was ruminating about something. Ruminating. Another word I learned in my trailer tutoring. Vocabulary drills.

"You still haven't answered my question," I said.

"I know. It's complicated."

"It shouldn't be. You either like something or you don't."

Ah, big mistake, I thought. *He hates binary thinking.*

"In other words," I said before he had a chance to respond and I could feel my heart picking up speed again, "you claim this big important task of yours is just a job, nothing more. But I'd bet deep down..."

My chest was beginning to heave, and my diaphragm pushed hard against my ribs, forcing my body to fairly bounce in place on the floor. Once again, I was hyperventilating, my lungs crying for oxygen, my brain in a vise. I remember wondering if my downstairs neighbor, Mrs. Kelsey, was home and might come up to check on me.

"…you…think this is…fun," I said before I blacked out.

Cilantro.

The lemony, bright scent of cilantro.

My eyes popped open. Several hazy images of the kitchen light fixture swirled around until they joined together and came into focus. The light was still on, and I had to squint.

My heart was beating normally as I sat up and looked around. I ended up with such a massive head rush that I had to grab the handle of the fridge and hold onto it until my equilibrium returned.

Where is Professor Peter Stone?

"Hello?" I called out. "Hello?" I couldn't bring myself to call him by name, like that would soil me somehow. It took a few minutes before I was relatively confident I could stand, so I scooted over to the chair where I had been sitting while he was cooking and pulled myself up into the seat.

There was my half-full Diet Coke and next to it was a DVD case with a folded note taped to it. I'm a fan of old movies, ever since I was in Hollywood, but I hadn't seen this one: *Helen of Troy*, 1956, Warner Bros.

I opened the note, which was written in elegant, cursive script that almost looked like it was written by a woman's hand. It said:

Kimber,

I'm not sure I would go so far to say what I do is "fun," but you are correct that I derive pleasure from it, which is the reason I've decided to take my leave. I'll have to call on you again some sunny day, but I can tell you that probably won't be for awhile. I have to straighten all this out with Atropos, who as you can probably guess, is <u>not</u> thrilled with me.

Until then, please enjoy this movie and the dinner I made. (Don't worry, I didn't poison it. ☻) Rossana Podesta was great as Helen. We talked about that role when I called on her. I still see her every so often, and we're great friends.

I'm hoping we will be, too.

In the name of our glorious father, Zeus…

Peter Stone

I folded the note and set it on the table next to the DVD case. My MacBook was at the other end of the table, next to my mail. I popped it and logged into my Gmail, but his email had disappeared. I logged into USF's website and did a keyword search for "Peter Stone."

Your search "Peter Stone" did not match any documents.

Not surprising, I guess. About what I expected.

I exhaled and then inhaled the cilantro again. *Mmmm. Hungry.*

The Pyrex dish was on the stove, still hot—despite the fact that it was now 3:37 a.m.—and covered with aluminum foil. I had been out for almost eight hours.

What was I going to do? Call the cops? I had no proof he even existed other than a note that looked like I had probably written it myself. Plus, I had the paparazzi to think of, and nobody wants to be labeled crazy in the pages of *Weekly World News*. I can see it now: "The Sad Last Days of Kimber Kaplan." Forget that, man.

So I grabbed a plate, served myself a sizeable piece, sat on the couch, and put on the movie.

Professor Peter Stone was right. Rossana Podesta was exquisite in that role.

And the sole was absolutely divine.

THE BORDERLAND

Columbus, New Mexico

Because Eli was short of stature, his words hung in the air over the dark-stained wood table and weren't dissipated by the ceiling fan overhead, though the vertical blinds next to the window whispered.

"Fuck it, man," he said with apparent resolve, staring at his words hovering by the ceiling. "I'm going to do it. I'm going to jump."

Kristi sat up on the wooden bench that, even as a kid, left her tailbone sore after extended periods of wolfing down Pancho Burgers and crinkle fries. Often with Eli.

She knew he was down, depressed since the recent passing of his grandmother in Palomas just across the border. He had smoked a lot of weed over the past few months and even used some peyote in a scrubby field on the other side of the border. Kristi hadn't been there for that, but heard his trip had been pretty intense.

He had never talked of suicide, though, even in jest.

This was new.

"Okay, look," Kristi said. "I know losing your grams sucked, but you've got so much to live for, and…"

"Like what?" he turned to her and spat, showing actual, serious, honest-to-goodness emotion, a departure from the norm for a really funny guy, perhaps the funniest Kristi had ever met. Which is one of the reasons, deep down, she loved him.

"I'm set up for a life working the fields, busting my ass for what? Minimum wage and a government that hates foreigners?" he said. "Trump thinks this place is a shithole; you know that."

"You're not a foreigner," Kristi broke in with just a tinge of derision that she hoped Eli wouldn't pick up on. "You were born here. You're an American citizen."

"Come on, don't be naïve. I may as well be a shitheel from across the border—or a drug dealer."

He grabbed the perfectly toned muscle of his left forearm from his work on the Davis ranch outside of town and pulled it, stretching a small tattoo of a crown with the words *El Rey* (The King) under it.

"Look at this dark skin," he said, loud enough that diners at nearby tables looked up. His eyes shifted toward them and then back to Kristi. Then he whispered, "This skin is going to stop me from going anywhere in this world. Can't go south because of the cartels. Can't go north because of the racism. Can't stay here because there's no opportunity."

Kristi said nothing.

"Look at you," he blathered on. "You got college in front of you, and maybe—probably—a job in Santa Fe or Albuquerque or, really, anywhere."

It was true. Kristi was headed to Las Cruces in the fall to study aerospace engineering at New Mexico State.

"You could go to school," Kristi said quietly, but even she didn't buy that. Eli's grades were shit, and they both knew it. He even rolled his eyes as if to say, *Come on, seriously?*

She went on, "I'm just saying, you can't give up no matter how much it hurts. The pain's going to go away, Eli. You have to believe that."

Eli leaned his back against the wood-paneled wall and laid his legs on the bench. "All I want to do is just…escape," he said. "Just escape all this."

"But what about me?" Kristi asked.

Kristi and Eli had been best friends since second grade after his family had moved from the chaos of inner city El Paso. They became fast friends, doing the things all little kids in Columbus did: riding their bikes, kicking around her orange-fluorescent soccer ball, enjoying Eli's grandmother's enchiladas when they were allowed to cross the border to Palomas. Over time, that friendship became love for Kristi and for Eli, too, she suspected, although they never discussed it. Ever.

But high school graduation was coming up fast, just a few months away. She studied hard in school and was awarded an academic scholarship to

NMSU. Eli didn't, though he was Deming High's best soccer player and had harbored an outside chance of an athletic scholarship somewhere. But that didn't pan out.

"Hon, you know you're my best friend," he said. "You're the only reason I haven't offed myself by now."

That didn't make Kristi feel better, though now Eli had turned his head and was staring at a black-and-white portrait on the wall of his ancestor Alberto, his high-cheeked grin and thick moustache flanked overhead by a shock of perfectly combed and shiny black hair staring earnestly into the future. Standing next to him was the one and only Pancho Villa, who'd led an invasion of Columbus in 1916. Alberto had been one of General Villa's top lieutenants and, according to Eli's grandmother, when the U.S. Army repulsed the invasion, Alberto never returned to Mexico.

"You're a legacy here, Eli," Kristi said, noticing his furtive stare at the portrait.

"What do you mean?" he replied, not looking at her, but out the window at Columbus's locally famous water tank standing stately behind the café.

"It means you've got history here, and you've got a responsibility to be part of it and add to it," she said. "You can't do that if you're…dead."

She didn't want to use that word. Damn.

He stared out the window a few seconds more and then turned toward her.   "Look, you know I ain't serious," he said, flashing a weak smile. If it were a little wider and a little more genuine, he'd look just like Alberto sans the moustache.

And she would have melted. It was that potent.

"I'm just going through a hard time," he said. "It'll pass. You know I can't leave you here. Who would make your life interesting?"

Their waitress strode up, lightly laid their bill on the table and said, "Whenever you're ready."

Eli smiled again, this time into a grin, and Kristi did, in fact, melt.

"I'm ready," he said.

They talked for another ten minutes about unrelated things, including the merits of attending Deming High's prom—as friends, of course—and then Kristi excused herself to use the bathroom. When she returned, the table was clean and wiped down, the condiments and napkins standing at attention. Even the bill was gone.

"He paid it," the waitress said, motioning toward the front door, but Eli was nowhere to be seen in the enveloping February darkness.

Kristi stepped with pep out the wooden front door and darted her eyes left to right and back again over the hoods of three cars that reminded her of tied-up horses in Old West movies.

Nothing.

What the hell…?

That's right—the water tank. Go. Go!

She fairly flew around the corner, but the encroaching darkness was too much. He had enough of a head start that she couldn't even hear running footsteps in front of her. She almost ran into a steel guardrail, which would have killed her shins.

And that's what he'd be doing too—running. Kristi may have been the moral and ethical voice of reason in Eli's world, but when he got an idea in his head, there was no talking him down. Kristi had often been caught up in the slipstream of his impetuousness.

But suicide?

"E!" she called out into the pitch. "Eli! Babe, don't do it!" She had never used a term of endearment with him before.

She reached one of the water tank's legs, and far above was the faint clip-clop of feet climbing ladder rungs. But heck if she knew how far up he was at that point. She'd never paid that close attention.

"Eli!" she yelled in the general direction of the footfalls.

Nothing.

A few seconds of self-loathing. Why the hell had she left him? He never paid the bill. Ever.

"Aaauugh!" came a voice far above Kristi and getting closer. Her eyes had adjusted to the darkness by now, and she could see the faint lines of her handsome man falling, falling, dressed in his ragged black *Los Tigres del Norte* T-shirt, jean jacket, and worn cowboy boots.

A blinding horizontal beam of light, so intense that she had to shield her eyes, which suddenly became vertical.

Eli was swallowed up in it.

Darkness again.

The cicadas chirped a long goodbye, and a meteor streaked across the stars.

Kristi was alone.

***

Silence! Deafening silence. When she collapsed, the stones cut into her legs and the palms of her hands.

She made herself small on the ground, huddling, her hands gripping her temples. A pebble stuck to her hand and pricked her temple, but she hardly noticed.

Her beloved. Gone. She was suddenly realized she felt a wartime widow.

Even though they had not married and she'd never even told him how she felt.

Silence. Deafening silence, drifting into the cold American night.

***

The meteor had barely disappeared when the beam of light returned, this time parallel to the ground and the scrub and gravel just beyond the steel traffic guardrail. It was horizontal for about a second before becoming vertical, now parallel with the water tank's legs, and as it did so, a figure of light stepped into the darkness.

He wasn't blazing, mind you. Like Moses' burning bush, he wasn't consumed by what appeared to be a sort of fire that didn't consume, though there was the smell of deep incense like the kind used in church that made Kristi's nose turn when she was a kid. Frankincense, maybe? What did was that other one—myrrh?

She hadn't been to church in years.

The light eventually dissipated and finally disappeared completely, leaving a man standing in its wake, burnished by whatever had delivered him here.

He was short, his hands on his hips, and he wore a white hat that looked akin to a fedora, though not exactly. His clothes were dark and formfitting, and he sported shiny black boots and a silver medallion supported by a thin chain. He was mustached, and bore a striking resemblance to…

"Kristi," he said in a deep voice.

Eli? Oh my God.

But he wasn't the same. He was older, maybe twenty-five or twenty-six, and had a cool, confident gait, as if he was…triumphant. That was it. He had achieved something, something deep and personal and ponderous.

Kristi fell backward and shook her head a little at the burning smell, which had started to fade, but was still notably pungent. Suddenly, she was on her backside, and she could hear the sound of a car engine turning over behind her.

"E-Eli?" she whispered.

"Yes, it's me."

"But, you just jumped like a second ago and…"

Eli took two giant steps and then knelt beside her, holding her hand.

"A lot's happened," he said. "We have much to talk about."

"But…"

He stopped her. "I saw Alberto," he said. "I've been with him all these years in his *hacienda* over there." He gestured toward Palomas before picking up a handful of dust and letting it sieve through his fingers. "This world, it's a mirror of the other, an imperfect reflection. This world is nothing but a valley of shadow.

"There it's everlasting peace where tribes live in harmony."

"You mean your Uncle Alberto?" Kristi said. "The one from the portrait inside the café?"

"The same. He is the patriarch of the Contreras tribe over there. He insisted I come back here, although I was reluctant to return to such an imperfect existence at first."

Okay, Kristi thought. *Did Eli spike my Diet Coke before I went to the bathroom? This is too much. He's like an adult or something. Mature.*

A man. Not a boy.

"I like to think so." Eli smiled and continued, "In the other world language is telepathic, and it's more…how can I say this without sounding guttural? Sensuous…like words aren't necessary, only feelings. You'll understand."

"What do you mean by that?"

"Alberto sent me to get you," he said, crossing his hands in his lap. "He knew I couldn't live without you."

And at that, a pinprick of light like a firefly formed behind him that began to shift horizontally and slowly wrap itself around them both.

About the Author

Gregg Voss works in public relations for an East Coast marketing agency during the day, covers high school sports for local newspapers most evenings, and is a prolific fiction writer in between. He has been a weekly and daily newspaper reporter and a trade publication editor in his career and has a master's degree from the University of Wisconsin-Milwaukee. He and his wife, Dorothy, and their daughter, Emmie, live in the Chicago suburbs. Visit GreggVoss.com.